SLUTS AND WHORES

short stories by C E Hoffman

ISBN-13: 978-1-945247-98-9

SLUTS AND WHORES

Copyright © 2021 by C E Hoffman

Edited by Cedric G! Bacon

First Edition, 2021. All rights reserved.

A Thurston Howl Publications Book
Published by Thurston Howl Publications
Lansing, Michigan

cedric.thurstonhowlpub@gmail.com

Cover by Sean Trayner

Printed in the United States of America

For Safe Space

You all changed my world

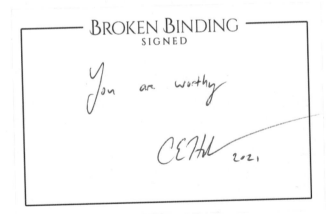

The following pieces were previously published.
Many thanks to those who gave my misfit toys an island!

"Nice Day to Get Laid" (poem)—*Punk Poetry* Magazine
"7-11" (previously published as "I Am Not a
7-Eleven")—*Maudlin House* Magazine
"Too Many Dreams"—*Trampsetters* Magazine
"My Right (Of Passage) (novel excerpt)"—
The Cliterature Journal
"I Am He"—*Litro NY* Magazine
"Dead Beth" (published as "Cotton Candy and
Graveyards")—*Dark Gothic Resurrected* Magazine
"Forget About Me" (previously published as "The
Intimacy Issue")—*The Weekenders* Magazine
"Fly, My Pretty"—*Vaughan Street Doubles* Magazine
"GTFO #1"—*Maudlin House* Magazine
"Between Lines/Legs"—*ppigpenn* Magazine
"Bloom (Blowjobs)" (poem)—*Pink Litter* Magazine

Table of Contents

"Prostitutes are people too."

—*Blair,* Gossip Girl

Nice Day to Get Laid*

Grown-up kid w/ groceries: cheese buns, Pepsi.
White clouds make chaos w/ sickgreen leaves.
The grass is not me, we
coexist separate-
ly.

Like how whores live alone no matter the number
of lovers they do (or don't) take home.
Like how mothers mourn while kids get to grow.
Like how whores live alone.

Grown-up girl w/ groceries: in-store sushi.
In other news, I'm making history.
In other words, I'm totally
FUCKED,
aka
damn lucky.

(*This title is a quote from Sex and the City. *Seriously.)*

7-11

SHE HAS A PACK of raspberry Pop Tarts and apple juice box for breakfast.

Last night was a bitch. (*One client, no tip*) Even worse, tonight, she's on a double shift. Hopefully, A** will let her order from the greasy spoon next to the massage parlour.

Eden knows she could do with some grease.

One adapts to upside-down days. Working from 3 am to 7 PM starts to make weird sense, like it's everyone else who's backwards, and it's only these rare, enlightened beings who get it.

Supply and demand is 24/7. It doesn't matter if it's 8 or 3 or 5, PM, AM, rain or shine. It may not be fair, but what is? Besides, it's better than waitressing.

Here, the customer is *never* right.

It's the noise alert that wakes her from what might have been a dream.

She kicks up her feet, tousles her hair, stands in line to be appraised (and hopefully picked).

A client! *Finally!*

Alas, he goes for the blonde too hot to work in a dive

like this.

Discrimination, that's what it is! Who says a gorg blonde is going to give a better handjob (*etc.*) than an honest-to-goodness girl-next-door brunette?

Ah well. Back to the couch. You'd think she'd be tired, but there's always a way to kill time.

Netflix, IG, Wish. Her phone's a best friend crooning, "Lean on me."

All her real friends live outside the city. What is there to do but work?

A parlour's a constant gamble. You might hit the jackpot or leave broke, and day to day, you never know.

All these stabs in the dark in the hopes of nailing paradise.

A** walks in. He is ridiculously nice to her, but every other girl says he's a jerk. She wonders where he hides his second face. What made him open a place like this? Was he desperate, greedy, curious?

"Eden, how are you?" His accent is hard to understand, but when in doubt, Eden always smiles.

"Hi, A**. Can I have my pay from yesterday?"

(Up-front pay is paid out the next day; tips, you keep. Rub n' tugs cost the guy forty up front; the girl keeps fifteen.)

He hands her a depressingly thin envelope from last night's bullshit. Ah well. There's always another day . . .

"Eden, can you stay late?"

"Huh?" She could have sworn she fell asleep, but her phone's in her hand playing Wheel of Fortune. Or something similar to it.

"That girl from B******* didn't get back to us. Stay until midnight?"

"Um . . ."

"11?"

"Well . . ." Eden wishes she were the kind of girl who had something to say. But she finds it's better when people speak for her.

"Time to make money!" A** encourages. Always smiling, just like Eden.

"Well, okay."

"Great. I'm getting coffee. You want anything?"

"Sweet potato fries from the diner, please?"

"Extra ketchup?"

"Always."

She binge-watches *Sense 8*; nobody comes in from 11 AM to 5 PM. Nobody who doesn't go for the blonde at least when, finally, at quarter to 6, a guy picks her.

Older men always go for Eden. She must boast an air of feigned innocence, a scent reminiscent of simpler days. This client usually smells like shit—sometimes literally—but thankfully he showered today.

Eden's not in the mood. She'd rather finish *Sense 8*, even though Netflix makes her no money.

She usually lets guys go pretty far whilst crossing her fingers for a good tip, but today, as his spiny fingers sneak their way to her precious treasure, she closes her legs.

He leaves a twenty, and no shame.

Ah well. There's always another horse to bet on, another guy to ride to the finish line.

As soon as she escorts Mr. Cheap to the door, a stranger takes her in.

He's younger, with one of those budding beer bellies, the kind of face that should know better.

She wonders what brings men in: divorce, death, boredom, loneliness? Are they that socially awkward, that salacious, that persistent a bachelor?

"Hi, honey, come on in." She grabs the towels. "Do you want to shower?"

"I already did."

"Great. I'll take you in here." Room 5 is her favourite. It seems more romantic. "Make yourself at home. I'll be right back."

She writes up the logbook, deposits the cash, pops a mint, applies extra deodorant, locks her phone, and says a prayer.

The prayer is a recent addition, and it feels silly, but:

> *"When with makeup my face I've adorned;*
> *When with jewels my body has worn;*
> *To the goddess who honours the whores;*
> *Bless us now,*
> *and ever more."*

It reminds Eden of that girl who worked for less than a week. Instead of flipping through a phone, she was always reading, and she told Eden that, once upon a time, prostitutes were sacred.

"We are conduits of the love goddess."

At the time, Eden called bullshit. But ever since that strange girl ditched her, Eden began to pray, a ritual which comes to its end when she reaches the assigned room. She knocks on the heavy door, always politely, always mechanically.

"Come in."

Her customer's naked on his stomach. The lights are dim.

Funny how so many guys' asses look the same.

She loves the hushed glow of this space. The delicate anticipation peppered with shy small talk. When she bends over and feels his eyes honour her body, she wonders if sex work was sacred all along.

All he wants is a hand job and eyes to gaze deep into when he cums. Eden is great at faces and noises, and he's done quick, melting all over her hands.

She passes him a towel and subtly disinfects her surprisingly sweaty palms.

They get dressed, make more small talk, her fingers crossed for a tip.

"How's the weather?"

"It's gorgeous. You should get out there."

"I'd love to. But I'm here 'til 11."

"Ah well." He ties up his shoes. "There's always another day."

He gives her a hundred and leaves through the back.

"Hi, Eden," says H****, the madam/receptionist. She's in for the evening. "A** says you're here until 11. That's great. Any chance you can stay a little longer? You can have a break."

"Hey, H****?" Eden can't believe she's saying this, but, "Can I talk to you?"

For some reason, she trusts H****. H**** doesn't smile like A**, but somehow that makes her seem nicer.

"Sure, hon. What's up? Did something happen with a customer?"

"No, nothing like that. But I'm kind of thinking of moving on."

H**** sits her down.

"Why? I thought you were making great tips."

"Tips are no good if no guy chooses you."

"What are you thinking of doing instead?"

The truth hits Eden upside the head.

Where could she go? How long could she last? Her savings are always running thin thanks to eating out all the time and ordering Uber, Lyft, and cabs instead of providing her own transportation.

"Backpage?" H**** guesses.

"Maybe?"

"Oh sweetie, that stuff is so dangerous on your own. Here, we look out for each other."

Eden thinks of all the times the blonde could have convinced a guy into taking them both for a double and didn't.

"Yeah."

"Obviously, do what you want. Just remember you have to give us two weeks' notice, and if you miss a shift . . ."

"I know. $500 fine." How could she forget? A** recites

the rules like they're the national anthem; H**** provides the backup chorus.

"I'm going to get coffee. You okay on your own? Gigi's still with a regular. He booked her for another hour!"

"Good for her." She wishes she meant it.

"Want anything?"

"Maybe later."

Ass back to couch, eyes back to screen.

The desk phone rings.

Eden answers. Weirdly disappointed, weirdly happy alone.

"A********, how can I help you?"

"Who's available?"

"Right now, we have . . ." She scans the schedule penned in bright, pretty pink:

3 AM-11 AM Eden, Brandy
11 AM-7 PM Eden, Gigi
7 PM-3 AM Bambi, Eden 7-midnight

". . . No one, actually."

"'Scuse me?"

"There's no one available. Our only attendant is with a customer."

"What about you?"

"I'm just visiting."

She hangs up, fixes her lipstick, packs her bag, and leaves through the front.

Backpage might be dangerous, but then again, what isn't? Nobody ever promised Eden paradise. If there is a heaven, she sure as hell isn't going to find it waiting for some guy to decide she's worthwhile.

And she's not going to waste any more time.

The End

You Only Die Once

SHE GAVE ME THE money, so I went down on her. Her friends watched from the pillows.

This was the furthest North I'd ever been. I knew Pretty People paid for sex (everyone does, one way or another), but had little desire to service them.

A good brain goes where the money is. A smart whore never follows her heart and always follows her head.

These girls were gorgeous. They would have surely tortured me in high school had they not been shipped off to boarding schools in Switzerland. Boney, manicured nails screamed glitter and decadence. Fat, shiny wallets made for promising tips.

Every eyelash could have set a castle on fire.

These girls were the bane of my pseudo-feminist existence, and here I was, literally on my hands and knees to please them.

Irony's a bitch.

My nose suffocated on her squirt sack. One of the prettier Pretties sat on my back and dragged her alligator claws down my spine.

Obediently, my skin bled.

My customer faked an orgasm; I pretended I couldn't tell. As I wiped my mouth, I wondered,

Why pay for a pleasure that's not real?

Hot blood danced on my skin. The roof party was a mess of loose pearls, writhing girls, gaudy diamonds, and ripped skirts; a blur of plastic, pawing perfection; mewing kittens flushed down the maw of a porcelain sink.

Drugs came and went like a politician's promises. Mucous membranes: glutted. Pretty pills and mountains of powder were huffed, puffed, sucked, blown, parachuted, swallowed, shot home.

My eyes carelessly combed the streets below. Pavement sneered up at me, reflecting old bursts of blood and beer. Little ants (allegedly humans) skittered on the concrete. Wind rustled bits of dust (that were really plastic bags.)

A line of taxis waited on the road: yellow cabs bleeding black on the sidewalk.

I trolled about, asked if anyone else wanted a go or a show. None were sober enough to answer. Jeweled eyes rocked in their skulls, sexy skeletons condemned.

Where went their dreams? Where were their parents?

I pitied them. At least the poor are honest in their poverty.

The sun went down, the sins ran out, my hours were almost up. I was the only one with a head on my shoulders instead of in outer space.

One last lady was lucid enough to thwart my escape. Raccoon eyes (thanks to cancerous paraffins) spasmed (thanks to all the drugs) on her diamond-bitten face (thanks to genetics, good nutrition, and a little surgery).

Her little, lithe limbs were dumb as jelly. Her hair was red hot. Its embers coiled around her face, reflecting the magma of her eyes.

"Leaving already?" she crooned. "Party's not over yet."

Gently, cautiously, I wove around her.

"I go where the money is, darling. No one else is willing to pay."

"I'll pay!" She fumbled in her bra for bills.

Funny how girls can arouse and exasperate you simultaneously. Wrists shaking, lip gloss flaking, she pressed several hundred-dollar bills upon my gawking lips.

"What do I have to do for this?"

"Nothing. I just want you to stay."

My dress (thanks to a thrift-store raid) was somewhere around my ankles (thanks to her friend who thought it'd be funny to fuck me with a champagne bottle. Thank god the glass didn't break.)

What did this part-time model with a head full of flame hope to find in me?

"Right." I grinned. "I'm your conversational whore, m'lady."

She grabbed my elbow, kissed my eyes, dragged me to the velvet beds. She said she wanted to kill me and bathe in my skin "like the Spartans did."

I liked her.

We talked until dawn. More accurately, she did. I listened as much as I could and spent the rest of the time admiring her hair.

Her lips made curious shapes against fading city lights.

The cabs left bloody trails of oil behind. The city went rowdy, then still. Later, in the dimmest morning light, stray pedestrians loitered in their loneliness. We witnessed the world upside-down, from the wrong side of the dawn.

It was strange going a whole night without hearing any sirens.

The girls were calm in the aftermath. They had aimed to get as fucked up as humanly possible, and in this, they succeeded. Now, they appeared appallingly Zen, blowing snot into fifty-dollar bills.

I thought of the money I'd make from bottling their sweat. Kids would be desperate for a spritz of these silky pheromones.

The redhead kept touching me. Her hands hurt, but not nearly as much as starving. I wondered where I could go to spend my night's (and morning's) earnings.

Ms. Red kept talking. She'd recite poetry, get high, kiss me, apologize. I was down for whatever but preferred to hear her talk.

It's better to be molested with thought.

The zenith spat twilight, purple, pink. The girls rose in unison, entranced by the twinkling sun. I realized they weren't on top of a building, but the world. Their daddies were kings, they princesses by proxy. They were the glue that stopped society from crumbling.

"Alright girls," the blondest Blonde declared, "Time to call it a day, wouldn't you say?"

I expected them to file out with wagging heads and coming hangovers but should have known these girls would go out with a bang.

One by one, they jumped. Their dresses became tails streaking far-off cloud. The whole sky was a rainbow of fabric, a flag of demise. A cover-worthy mass suicide.

High fashion briefly became literal.

I said one of those dumb things people say in the face of surreal tragedies:

"Wait!"

My ankles snapped. I clamoured off the cum-stained silk to catch skirts as I might grab the wings of birds.

"What the hell are they doing?!"

Red smiled, which, considering the circumstances, I found inappropriate.

Several kamikaze killjoys remained on the roof, and try as I did to impede their flighty suicides, they, too, jumped to make Pretty Pancakes for breakfast.

Soon, it was only us two.

I spun. Sick in brain, wet in skull. There was an odd disease in me, the plague of mortality, one I hadn't noticed until surrounded by fatal woes.

Lady Red cracked her neck.

"Don't fret, my dear. You're prettier when you smile."

"How would you know? I haven't smiled once tonight!" I leaned over the edge and winced. "It's awful."

"No," she corrected, "it's wonderful!"

Her toes dabbled in a pirouette; she must have taken ballet as a kid.

"Don't!" I lunged for one of her knees. "Please. Don't leave me all alone."

"You sweet thing! If only I could explain. Dying is fabulous! We make a point of doing it as often as possible."

Had they slipped something into my drink?

"It started with cocaine. So many good stories start with coke, don't you think? We were convinced that, if we jumped, we'd fly off and lay waste to the tar sands." Her grin was nostalgic and eerily wise. "Of course, no girls grow wings. We fell and died, like anyone else. But . . . we woke up. New faces. New bodies. New lives to waste."

Screams from early risers erupted from the street.

"Of course," she admitted, "like anything worth doing, jumping is a gamble. All jump, but not all are reborn. Who knows!" She craned her fantastic jawline. "This leap could be my last!"

I kissed her. Hands wild, passion useless, I hoped to find truth beneath sex.

For once, I tried to think with my heart instead of my head.

"Forget this." My nails pulled at her but couldn't reach within. "Come live with me."

She grabbed both my hands like she wanted to dance.

"Why don't *you* come die with *me*?"

The strongest temptations are also strangest.

Despite my heart, her head, her lips, I wouldn't play Russian Roulette with gravity.

When she jumped, she jumped all alone: red clashing with blue.

All I could dare to do was look down.

The End

Poppy's Game

WANT WHIMSICAL!"

The doll said this and stared. She had a peach face with pink cheeks and red lips and blue eyes like hot, happy marbles.

I loved her. She was the best friend there could ever be.

"What do you want to play?" I asked.

We were in the attic. The doll liked to play there. The dust wrinkled my nose and got stuck in my brain.

The doll always liked my brain.

Her glass eyes juggled possibilities. Then painted lips mutated into a hot, happy grin. It reminded me of cough syrup.

"I want to play . . . the suicide game!"

I shook my head. Somewhere, floorboards creaked.

"Mom says we're not allowed to play that anymore."

The nauseous smile flopped into a frown. A wet, wiggly frown.

"Why not?"

"Mom says it scares her to find me dead. . . . She thinks I fake it, you know. She thinks I do it to scare her." After some consideration, I added, "She doesn't like you."

Beaded eyebrows fell on her pretty forehead.

"I don't like her, either," the doll said.

I changed the subject. "What would you like to play instead?"

"We could play . . . we could play . . ." The smile went up, but the eyebrows stayed down. "The murder game! I want to play the murder game!"

"How do you play?"

She rocked back and forth. Her porcelain hands moved together to clap but couldn't touch.

"It's like the suicide game, only outwards!"

"I don't understand."

"Don't worry. I'll teach you. First, we have to find someone to play with."

I had the doll under my arm when I came down the stairs. Mom was in the kitchen finishing a beer with breakfast. Some of the smelly liquid dribbled off her chin.

Mom glared at the doll. The doll glared back.

"I hate that thing. Get rid of it!"

"Please, Mom, don't make her mad."

Mom had already seen what the doll could do, and I knew she was too scared to do anything.

I felt bad, but I couldn't say goodbye to my only friend. The doll was there for me more than mom ever was.

"I want you *alive* when I pick you up from school, you hear?" she laughed, but it was the angriest laugh I ever heard. "Christ, you love driving me crazy, don't you?"

I went for the door.

"Wait, I'll drive you."

"No." I told her. "You're too drunk to drive."

I had the doll under my arm at school. My teacher kept looking at me. He was always looking at me. Every time he did, I got a knot in my tummy that stayed tight all day. The chalk screamed on the blackboard, and the white burned the green. The world went blurry, then I blinked, and everything was clear.

The doll whispered answers to me.

When it was time to go home, the teacher asked me to stay.

The doll was cuddled in my armpit. I knew she didn't mind; she said she liked the taste of my sweat.

My teacher knelt in front of me. He always sat and stood close enough I could smell what sandwich he had for lunch. Today, it was ham and mayonnaise.

It should have made me feel special, but I only felt scared.

The doll told me take a step back, but I couldn't move.

"Why do you always have that doll?" asked my teacher.

I clutched it, afraid he'd take her.

"Am I in trouble?"

"You shouldn't bring a doll to school," he said, chest heaving. "It's too . . . adorable."

I wanted to run.

His hands trembled. They reached out and touched my elbows, too gentle to be trusted.

"Put it down."

All I wanted was to get in bed with the doll in my arms. My dreams would make everything okay. I wanted to smell dirt and dust and darkness, to chase butterflies and pin them on my dress.

"Put down the doll."

He took my friend and put her on his desk. She faced us, eyes ready to slice.

"Please, let me have it . . ." I reached. Unless the doll was at my side, I remembered how wrong the world was.

The teacher grabbed my chin so I would look at him. It didn't hurt, but I started to cry. It was like the hurt was going somewhere I didn't know, somewhere on the inside I couldn't see.

"Be quiet, or I will never give your doll back."

I looked at the doll. Her mouth was wide, glaring and agape. She trembled on the desk, knocking over the teacher's pens.

I looked at his watch. It looked bright and sharp, like it could cut me. Then I looked up at him, and it looked like he might cut me too.

My face was on fire. My nose dripped all over my lips.

I could see the doll over his shoulder, eyes burning red and wild.

The teacher didn't see.

He was too busy doing things that made me want to scream.

We were in the attic. Its musty browns and muddy blacks laughed at me. I had a sneeze held up inside, and it wouldn't come out no matter how hard I tried. The doll watched me from her box, plastic tears tumbling out of her innocent face.

"I'm so, so sorry," she said, and I knew she meant it.

I cried quietly so Mom wouldn't hear. I had a flu no medicine would fix. This was a nightmare I would never forget.

"I should tell someone," I said between sobs.

The doll creaked her delicate neck.

"Nobody will believe you."

"Then what do I do?"

Her porcelain turned to steel.

"Didn't I tell you I'd teach you how to play?"

I didn't go to school the next day. The doll and I napped outside until the bell rang. Then we walked to class, holding hands.

My teacher was there, whistling. My shoes scraped the floor, and he looked up.

"Oh, hello Poppy. We missed you in class today."

I frowned; I remembered a book that showed all the

different monsters in the world. My teacher was a monster, too, but he was the worst sort of monster.

He was a human.

The doll hissed in my armpit. I put her down.

The teacher walked towards me but only after shutting all the blinds. He reached over my head to shut the door.

Sweat tap-danced all over my hands. I was sick again.

The doll's face was the perfect blend of a grin and sticky-sweet smile, like the pictures on the boxes of Band-Aids. She nodded for me to approach. I did, hands behind my back.

My teacher's pants were wrinkled and brown. I gazed at his blushing face, and for the first time in my little life, I understood hate.

Hate was the most wonderful thing I ever felt.

He knelt down, like the doll told me he would. I wanted to retch, but I waited like the doll told me.

Huge, hairy hands crushed my shoulders, making it so hard to breathe.

"I was thinking about yesterday. Were you?"

I nodded.

The teacher closed his eyes, lips pursed like an ugly fish.

"Now!" the doll squealed with fury and delight.

I took the scissors from behind my back and pushed them as hard as I could into his neck, exactly where the doll taught me. When I pulled them out, thick, red streams shot out of the teacher's skin. He gargled and bubbled at the mouth, holding where I'd poked him, staring at me with confused, trusting eyes.

"Poppy?"

"Again!" the doll cried.

I jumped and gasped and brought the scissors down, the silver blades slathered in blood. I missed the teacher's neck and stabbed his nose instead. He fell on his back. When he did, I stomped all over the parts he'd made me kiss. I then took my scissors, raised them high, and watched when the bloodstained blades disappeared into his chest.

Somewhere beside me, the doll cried, "Play with him! Play with him!"

My fingers were weak, my knuckles exhausted, but I kept stabbing him.

Somehow, my doll gave me strength.

He never fought back. All he did was stare, blood squirting out of so many holes, turning my name into a moan.

"Poppyyyy..."

The blood was a big, smelly, gushy spill. It stained my blue dress purple.

I rolled down my socks and kicked off my shoes, leaving bloody footprints.

The doll's shrieks faded into giggles. She rocked back and forth, back and forth, hands not quite close enough to clap.

"Again! Again!"

We were alone now. There was nothing of my teacher left.

I thought I'd be scared to leave The Big City, but this new place looked the same. The trees smelled the same, and flowers had the same colours, and the sun set in the same place.

I sat on a bench. The doll and I stared at the lake ahead, toes hanging over our seats.

There was a man behind me. I could see him through the back of my head. He wore a big, brown hat, and a long, brown coat, and he stared at me.

I hated him. Something about his smile made me sick again. The doll's eyes curled. She whispered, "He's sick."

"Has he got the flu?"

"He's sick in the brain. Sick like your teacher was."

Icicles kissed my spine. For a moment, everything went white. I couldn't see, couldn't feel anything.

The man wove his way around the bench and knelt before me.

"Hello little girl. Are you lost?"

His stretchy fingers teased my knee, tracing my cotton tights.

"Do you need me to help you find your parents?"

I touched my hand to his. He looked up, and I saw the doll was right; his eyes glimmered with disease. The doll looked up at me and down at the man, smiling.

I tugged his pinkie with my fist. My smile matched the doll's so well, you could hardly tell who was who.

"Would you like to play with me?"

The End

First Date Nº1

"I'm trying to change my Bed Karma."

—*Miranda,* Sex and the City

THE GIRLS WERE SKINNY with nice personalities and high-waist jeans.

The boys were a little awkward, and I was, of course, between.

We pretended it wasn't a date, but he held my waist while I headbanged.

When you can have anyone, it's hard to want anything.

His bracelet was made of lava beads. And he touched my hand. And the boys sang.

Boys sing about starting bands. Girls wish they did.

I wish I dropped acid. I wish my boobs fit this bra. I wish we would explode in LOVE right NOW, if not through a kiss, through this; that is, living.

Life screams, clatters, clamours. I am the most beautiful boy in the world. Someone says, "Free beer is the best . . . beer;" Jordan says, "You wake up, you fuck, you die," but I would love to LIVE.

He had a shaved head, uncircumcised dick, big hands, bigger heart, and his eyes . . . his eyes, his eyes, his eyes were hazel (grey most of the time).

I am not a hot mess, but I'm a mess, and it's hot. I wish I could take my shirt off. Wish my psychic skills read like street signs, 'cause tomorrow is mine but I never know what it brings.

Tomorrow, I will wake up, give a boy a blowjob, discover I've lost my credit cards, go blonde, and find my MasterCard in Jung.

I will sit with the boy in the shade. We will kiss, and he will smoke while we discuss the joy of summer flings, 'cept the one thing I omit is my last "fling" lasted 5 years plus a pregnancy, but then again I'm a different Me, so maybe I can do this differently.

The Beginning

Too Many Dreams

VICKY WAS A TWENTY-YEAR-OLD Business Major who didn't believe in ghosts until a '68 Jeep Cherokee parked itself on her lawn.

Vicky lived in one of those charmingly dilapidated house shares between the University and the North Side. The house came with one and a half bathrooms and three roommates: one Physics Major, one Pre-Med, and one Artier-Than-Thou Music Theorist.

Vicky swallowed her pride, paid rent ($515, plus internet), and kept the heck to herself.

The Big City was only a means to an end. Yet as the days lingered and the piles of dishes piled higher, the end to Vicky's means seemed further and further away.

Vicky was losing sleep. Even worse, she was remembering dreams, at times so vividly she'd wake in an elated, traumatized sweat.

Vicky didn't believe in dreams. All she wanted was a rich-bitch, Instagrammable existence free of sententious housemates, lucid dreams of soaring eagles, and other poignant BS, and especially jeeps that drove themselves to your front door and stayed there.

There was no question who the jeep came for. Surely as they'd seen it mosey onto the property, guzzle contentedly, and click its engine off, they knew it came for Vicky.

All the work she'd done to keep her head down all the way to Top Honours, shattered by some lousy rezjeep.

The jeep SCREAMED rez. Shabby hood. Tree-bashed vents. License plate drowned in mud. Years of abuse, misuse, love, hunting trips, camping trips, teenage trysts, car accidents, all rubbed and kneaded in like fresh bannock.

A past not even hers.

And it still came back to haunt her.

After the third day, her roommates got nervous.

"Are you gonna get rid of it?" Trust-Fund-Rockboy asked.

"It's. Not. Mine!" she'd insist, stomping upstairs with the Business Section.

Oh, but it was. Nobody else could go near it. Ms. Smart-n-Pretty fell back five feet when she attempted to approach. The car wasn't violent, per-se, but made it clear Ms. Smart-n-Pretty was extraneous.

Mr. Nobel-Prize-Wannabe beseeched the jeep with peaceful tidings; the jeep spat oil in his face (but was kind enough not to leave a stain). Trust-Fund-Rockboy wouldn't go near the damn thing.

Neither would Vicky.

"Please, Vicky, reason with it!" Too-Smart-Too-Pretty begged her one day over oatmeal and blueberries.

"It has nothing to do with me!" Vicky declared one more time.

But college kids know a lie when they hear one.

There was nothing Vicky wanted in that jeep. Nothing pure, nothing safe. She could smell pain a mile away, and that jeep reeked of it.

Eventually, everyone caves to their destiny.

Vicky went to talk to the jeep on Friday.

She cleared her throat. Next step would've been a handshake. Alas, this encounter required intimacy.

Lights hummed to life. The exhaust pipe coughed awake. Vicky stood firm; she knew her roommates were window-watching.

"Are you a ghost, jeep?" (What else could she say?)

The voice that answered filled her bones like gold or honey.

"No, I'm not a ghost-jeep. But it was better than hitch-hiking!" The driver door opened, and out stepped nothing, yet Vicky swore she heard confident feet grace the grass.

She'd never felt more at home, or afraid.

Noise on the hood: an affectionate pat. The jeep purred: a giant, domestic cat. Vicky refused to believe she was seeing or feeling—any of this.

She only wanted to return to watching stocks.

"I don't know what you're looking for . . ." Her throat shook. "But it's not me."

"Oh, but it is!" The voice was warm, and welcoming. Vicky wished it would go away. "Only you can help me."

"I can't. And even if I could . . ."

The slamming of the jeep door severed her sentence. Inside the house, she heard Trust-Fund-Boy shriek.

"Listen!" the voice commanded, still soft, but stronger. "You may not have ended up in a ditch, but some of us did!"

The voice tampered with what Vicky valued most: her boundaries.

She felt her walls crumbling.

"I'm not what you think. I'm a Business Major. I'm a nobody!"

Vicky wondered how a ghost could sigh.

"Do you really think I'd drive all the way here if I didn't know you're the one?"

Few could deny truth when it stared them in the face.

"What do you need?" she dreaded the answer. Revenge? Blood? Where would this take her?

"Clothes."

". . . Pardon me?"

"Clothes! An unmarked grave is bad enough. The least I could get is clothing."

"That's it? You just want . . . clothing?"

"I'm not saying it'll fix everything . . ." Again, that sigh, perfect for TV. "But it's a start."

Vicky ran, slamming the door in her hurry.

"Something blue would be nice!" the ghost called after her.

"Oh my god, did it kill you?"

"Is it leaving?"

"Are you hurt?"

Vicky ignored her roommates' concerns, jumping three stairs at a time. She tore into Trust-Fund-Boy's ironically immaculate room. He pursued her downstairs and not-so-eloquently told her what he thought about people who barged in. She pushed past, his brown, leather, red feather fedora in hand.

Whatever his whines of protest, she was too fast to hear them and swung to the upper flight of stairs, where three other rooms remained. ("Are you okay?" "What are you doing?"—more questions ignored.)

Those chocolate brown khaki pants, she decided, would be Nobel Prize's donation; Too-Smart's cobalt top would pamper the pile.

She paused in her own room, not from indecision, but sentiment: a feeling far rarer than dreams.

Contrary to Trust-Fund's closet, Vicky's was unabashedly haphazard. Under the stew of dog-eared textbooks and missing shoes sat a lonely cardboard box longing to be touched.

Vicky pulled out the brown leather jacket her father once wore roaring down open highways, sleeves worn with so many dangerous memories. Kisses. Concerts. Beers.

Car accidents.

She buried her face in it and breathed for what seemed like a long, long time.

Then she ran outside.

The End

The Horror of Zen;

MAYBE THE SOUND OF a fridge. A falling calendar could wake you up. You may or may not realize fame's a train that long pulled out of the station and all's left is notoriety/ bullshit which might be fine, depending what you're going for.

I woke up from my calendar coming off the wall 'cause I hung it with green paint tape 'cause the tacs won't go through. I dunno if it's my wrists or this baby mausoleum's got concrete behind the drywall.

No, I didn't kiss her, but I canceled my hair appointment. Winter came back the night before last, and you know I'd keep on with this, but it hurts.

FINE, I'll keep on it, but only 'cause I love you and you are just as scared as me. What happens when we run out of ink, days, words? Don't'cha dread the unbelievable beauty of silence and how little it hurts?

Pain is the lifeline. Remove it, and you erase modern life. Match me with a war-torn Europe, a stock market crash, some crazed totalitarian in a toupee who is most certainly misunderstood. We are fear mongers. We suckle the tit of bullshit, birth all these idiots and breed uncertainty, lies, walls, isolation, (in)security.

You don't want me to say I love you or you're worth it. Where's the struggle? Where's the bullets?

No wonder so many swallow; we are a sad sea of gaping holes.

No, I didn't kick her out. In the long run, she did that to herself.

Never trust a feminist who wears red lipstick. The darker the shade, the closer you gotta watch them. She will drag you to protests, drag you into bed and suck you dry, and not in the good way.

No, I'm not a misogynist. I didn't assault her dignity (if she had any to begin with). No man, she needed a place to stay, that's it.

You were there. Why ask? I'm telling ya: better drop those bitches.

No, I don't hate them. They're victims of circumstance, like everyone in this damn city, like everyone on this damn planet. That's what I mean, man. I have a home; my parents loved me. Nobody wants to hear that! We want riches so we can waste them. We want to be famous and left the fuck alone.

You may not understand this, kid, but whores are human. Whores are actual living, breathing, shitting persons with faults and aspirations. Whores can laugh and cry and fret over pimples and cellulite.

Once upon a time, whores ate at Denny's before the electricity fried. Once upon a time, whores were addicted to wi-fi and knew how to change tires because they ran a renovation business one time.

Believe it or not, Johns are people, too, who breed dogs, have kids, and some even tip.

We've made a world of war zones. Good and bad, Us and Them.

Division should be left to Math and in our heads.

I know what her friends will say. Lackeys are locusts; they feed on misery. They gorge like the starving would on bread. I don't care what they say; I didn't go to that rally to pick up chicks. Believe it or not, even the jaded give a shit. I have to meditate every day to stay remotely sane and wear steel toes everywhere not as a dyke flag—I just *like* it.

There's something to be said for a life of love and caring, for being fed, handed opportunities. I'm not dissing her for revoking all that WASPy privilege. If I had parents like that, I'd bail, too. She was due her freaky, fucked up, slutted out, hyper-liberal white guilt. But I mean, you saw her at that party. You know what I'm talking about. What's the difference between a see-through dress and a cry for help?

I'm not trying to get into your business. I'm not saying DON'T date her ... I'm not even saying she's a bitch. All I'm saying is you better watch it.

'Cause you may wake up from something, fucking foghorn on the water, your upstairs neighbour's dog, rain pounding on the window desperate to get in, or even—I dunno—a calendar falling, and I tell you it'll be louder than any bomb, more brutal or shocking than any assault rifle or assault.

And you may or may not see in the grip of your childish fears that all those horror movies, war movies, action flicks, and violent anal porn have been very effectively and subtly slicing you into submission. It won't matter if the phone rings or a little girl screams on the street because you will be numb waiting for something real while the real war is on all the while in your mind.

The worst part is you'll ignore the deepest bits, the pinching "No" in your guts you ignored when she asked to stay the night.

The End

The Peace of Pain;

GOOD GOD, SON, DON'T *ruin your road trip over a girl.*
You were right: I should have never dated her. I
should've been a monk, but it's too late for religion.

It's time to get away.

We're all psychos now. I'm glad to be one with the world.
We're driving, and we'll drive as far as we can and see what
happens when we stop.

Merry brought soda cans and Gerry cans. Tim brought
a backpack full of mushy peas (in cans). We knew to avoid
the overpass 'cause it's jammed, but Merry knew a back road
through the ravine.

It's like we forgot the trees. There're actual living, live an-
imals in there! I told Merry to floor it, I was so freaked. We
drove and drove, gravel smacking like so many machine guns,
and that was when I got what you said about the war being
on the inside.

We drove and drove. It was like the trees followed. Five
trunks kept our pace the whole time.

I felt crazy again, and I liked it.

We drove and drove. Trees battled the sky.

The sky won.

I went really raging mad then. Wondered why people wrestled with whether or not God exists. Isn't God obvious? Wasn't it God I saw when the night sky stole the trees? When all this sparse space, this ugly beauty, exploded in my face like I was coming up for air.

I wish you were there. You could've told me.

I thought we'd never get out of the Big City; I thought nobody ever could. But I knew as soon as we left, we would never get back in. That was it. We're doomed to an eternity of tinny peas in crushed cans, which feels okay. I'm sure that'll change when I go BAD insane, the crazy that's a lack of happy rather than an excess. I'll go THAT kind of crazy soon enough, and that's when I'll hallucinate her hitchhiking on the road.

You said, *"Never trust a feminist who wears red lipstick,"* and you were right, but you should never trust a dyke who gives good advice, and that's you, my friend.

That's you.

The End

The Lie of Reality.

OF COURSE, YOU'RE OKAY. You're the centre of the universe, for god sake. You dare to don leopard panties under a shrink-wrap mini that may actually be made of cellophane.

You are the Beauty AND the Beast, and bear both bare to the world.

I tell you this not because you never knew it, but because you need to be reminded, what with the looming rent and MIA roommates.

When people say, *"It'll Be Okay,"* or, *"It Gets Better"*, it rightly sounds like bullshit, but I do not embark to smother you with platitudes. I am only interested in facts:

1. You Are Strong
2. You never meant to lead him on
3. You'll get through this.

These are verified.

How do I confirm a fact when it has yet to happen? Simple; I'm outside of Time.

Time complicates things. Outside of time, the world is easy, bright, and clean. Out here, it is clear to see your stressors are temporary.

I am not your guardian angel. You are not quite special enough to have one. But you are special to me. I know you have seven pairs of shoes, two dresses, three names. I know your red lipstick is too dark for your face. You have fucked up a bunch, and you're sorry, and it's okay.

Don't believe me? Repeat:

I Am Okay

Everything always works out for me

I Am Safe

The universe is friendly.

These are trial-run, seal-approved, professionally certified certainties. Whether or not you believe in them, facts persist. Repeat them enough times, and you'll begin to see, hear, think, taste, and feel reality. You may even for a moment slip outside of time, and then we just might meet.

Until then, I send you my love.

As ever.

As always.

The End

Fun Farm

YOU GOTTA TRY THIS APP, IT'LL
CHANGE YOUR LIFE, I SWEAR!!!

DID YOU KNOW 80% OF ALL ADULTS REPORT
HIGH RATES OF DEPRESSION AND ANXIETY?

FUN FARM IS HERE!

AND IT'S HERE TO STAY!

LET US TAKE YOUR PAIN AWAY!

CHANGE YOUR SAD TO GLAD!

JUST A CLICK- IT'S THAT EASY!

DOWNLOAD FUN FARM TODAY!!!

F*cking ads! I thought I shut them off.
I check my Settings to find they've reset AGAIN:

INSTANT DIRECT DOWNLOAD - ALL - ON

I shut them off AGAIN:

DIRECT DOWNLOAD - ALL - OFF

Clicking OFF fifty more times for good measure.
Like it'll make a difference.

Everyone said to get the latest update because it made banking more efficient. Nobody warned about the direct download subscription. Call me old-fashioned, but I like dreaming dreams, not ads.

They were right; it's much more convenient. Besides, it's not like your phone's inside your mind. It's merely abreast of its happenings; it collects information, so you don't have to worry.

Despite this, I worry all the time.

Direct deposit's great, and so are menus that know what I want based on the composition of my stomach acid, but I cannot condone corporate-sponsored bullsh*t.

. . . I REALLY hate the automatic censorship.

The windows creak open to let in all that fresh air so many fear. I breathe long and deep just to piss off all the people who aren't there.

Above, I witness today's first wave of balloons: our nation's favourite pastime. It started as a way to get rid of the birds, but that was before people realized how fun it was.

I close the windows.

Di is awake in the kitchen, screen-splitting between *Grand Theft Auto 180* and an essay. It looks like they're in the same spot I left them last night.

My little sibling is eleven years younger than me, and since our mom and dad are very dead, that elects me as pseudo-parent. I suck but do my best.

◉   ◉   ◉

Di is a genderf*ckfluid panqueer and very proud of this identity, which they amassed when they were four-and-a-half.

Di's always been an outlier.

Their version of good morning:

"Everyone's zee-cray for Fun Farm."

I wipe off the table; they raise their elbows when necessary.

"Is that so?" I say.

"It's so. Demand's so high, they're hosting job fairs everywhere."

"Everywhere as in here?"

"Auto-totes, sib." I see my sibling's eyes for the first time in a week. When they look at me, I have that strange, sudden terror I've missed something, or that I'm going to if I don't act fast.

When they look at me, I sense they might be feeling the same thing.

"Can I go?" Di asks.

"To the job fair?"

"Aut. Oh. Totes."

I pour them a glass of electrolytes; they down it in one impressive chug and are back in their head, on their screen, flicking through pages with their eyes.

"Why?"

"'Cause I want a job!"; their eyes move too fast for me to keep up.

"Again, I ask, why?"

"Everyone wants a job!"

"I don't!"

"That's 'cause you already have one, le duh!"

"To ensure our rent is paid and you stay hydrated. There's no need for you to get one, too. I want you to focus on your education!"

"But all my education's here!" By "here," they mean "their head" and the screen attached to it. "I'm speeding through my courses. I'll grad in a year, eaze."

I measure their words like I'm Anubis. They further their case:

"Pleeeease! It'll be an adventure! The Fun Farm has this hyper-lit factory on the cuuuutest island off the south coast. Internships are as short as three months! You won't even know I'm gone, and then I'll be back with a boatload of zeroes in our account . . ."

"Whoa, whoa, wait. A literal IRL factory? No way. Everything's remote! I got my Psych degree sitting on my a**. Literally."

"Times are a-changing, sib. Fun Farm needs people to work with their *hands*. Micro-chip polishing, stuff like that."

"Sounds stimulating."

"For the wallet, anyway. What do I care about my brain? Brains don't bring anything but problems. And those are the very problems Fun Farm wants to fix."

To demonstrate, my sibling opens the app.

It's the first time I've seen Fun Farm in action, though I've been attacked by its campaign for weeks. I've nearly caved just to see WTF is up but can now live vicariously through Di's download and the bright shadows it projects on their face.

It's charming, I'll give it that: quaint landscape, rolling hills, some farm that resembles a ten-year-old's idea of the Alps. Mountains cascade in the background, with blithe, idiotic sheep in the fore. The sun is so warm, I can feel it all these feet away.

Floating in the clouds: a juicy red button begging to be pressed.

CHANGE YOUR SAD TO GLAD!

YOUR MAD TO RAD!

YOUR PAIN TO A-OKAY!

YOUR AGONY TO ECSTASY!

"Watch, watch, it's hyper-lit."
Di plugs in. The app reads their mood as "Meh."

CHANGE YOUR MEH TO YEAH!

The button is pressed.

My sibling's eyes fizzle from their usual apathy into nothing short of a fit. Pupils dilate, mouth makes way for a brash, obnoxious laugh, and they leap to their feet, ready to take on the world and everybody in it.

"Yeahhhh!" they bounce about in a happy burst. I wonder what Mom and Dad would think. "It'll swap anything you want to get rid of, from meh to bleh to kill-me-now into the best of the best of the best! Yeahhh!"

Serotonin ebbs. Vein at temple pulses. Di collapses in a good way. Mood-meter reads:

CONTENT

"You gotta try it, sib. Just once. It'll change your life. I swear."

I'm late for work.

Sometimes, I get so mad, I don't know where the anger can go. A button would be too weak to mute my rage. My anger burns holes in my stomach called ulcers. My panic stirs storms in my head, making migraines.

I understand Fun Farm's appeal. If society grants no space for one's more challenging emotions, escape becomes your only option.

As for me, my only option is work.

I walk. We had to sell the car and can't afford the airtrain. Yet.

It's a nice day. The second wave of balloons (this time red) mask the sky like a shower in reverse. It is so achingly beautiful, I almost forget about clouds.

Everyone's headphones are in, their speakers are on, their eyes on their screens because their screens watch out for them. Life is so hands-free, people sometimes forget how to use them. Society is the safest it's ever been. Who are we to complain?

Yet, I wonder if people are so much content as compla-cent. I seldom witness passion, creativity, or bliss. That "Yeah" on Di's face was the closest to a real, raw emotion I'd seen in weeks (Apart from in my own addled brain).

That's why I wanted to be a psychologist; I longed to in-spire the masses to feel.

But that didn't pay.

I ring the doorbell of the massive pre-war penthouse, an archaic monstrosity which belies the sleek apartments flank-ing it on either side.

This place is a romantic step outside time, much like the person residing.

The doorbell rings back; I'm let in. You'd think I'd have a key by now, but above all, Sel values privacy.

Sel has been my "employer" for five years. She demands much but pays well, and often in cash—a precious commod-ity, ultimately untraceable, and great for squaring debts.

Sel is strange. Strangest of all is she uses zero technolo-gy. She boils pots of water, sure, but goes little beyond that. She doesn't own a phone, doesn't listen to jingles, preferring instead to sing acapella, dancing all around her giant house and filling up space with song. It's weirdly wonderful.

Sel's a book keeper. Literally; she keeps books, allegedly because nobody else wants them, but I think she has a soft spot for turning their pages. Testing their weight. Enjoying their colours and smells.

As for me, I have a soft spot for being able to afford both clothes and meat.

Yes, sex is included in my job description, but she mostly likes company, and I like supplying it.

In bed, she plays with my hair.

"Everyone's mad about this Fun Farm app," I report.

"I've heard." She feigns disinterest, but I know she gets a tingle from these facts of the outside world where everyone swipes their lives away. She considers our country a car wreck, and while she averts her gaze, still enjoys updates on the accident.

Usually, her silver hair falls over her eyes, which is a shame; she has the most beautiful eyes.

"Di wants to work for them."

"And will you let her?"

"Them," I correct. "And I'm not sure."

Her breath is hot honey in my ear.

"Best to steer clear of Society. Believe me."

"Spoken like a true recluse!"

She smiles at that. I smile back but have to ask, "How has the world wronged you, that you lock yourself away from it?"

I've asked her this question far too many times. Today, I'm surprised to get an answer.

"The world is not Society, and Society is not the world. It is Society who has done me wrong, and Society, I scorn. Not that they care about me. To them, I don't exist!" She laughs like not-existing is a good thing.

It seems she was running her whole life, until she decided to stop. What is she doing now? Hiding?

Yes, hiding. Which is why I must protect her.

Then again, her money is a better guard than I could ever be. All I can offer is this.

I watch her light up an ancient cigarette in an even older cigarette holder.

"Would you tell me about the war again?"

She blows smoke on me; it smells like memories.

"Goodness, no! Why do you dwell on such things?"

"It's always on my mind. And nobody ever talks about it. Except you. And my parents. But they're dead."

Sel lies on her back and sighs at the ceiling. I know what she's thinking: "You're no fun today."

"It was a dangerous time. Just be glad you weren't alive."

"I'm not so sure I'm glad to be alive now!"

"Oh, hush!" she whispers my name like it's a magic word from one of her books. "You're always so worried: about what to do, what people think. Where's that wild, gorgeous girl I once knew? The one who would throw around books quoting Jung when she was drunk?"

I trace the spine of her prettiest book, the one about a wrinkle in time.

"She had to grow up."

Self-growth can only be found via responsibility. What does it mean for our development if we always choose the quick fix?

Less content, more clicks.

Less feeling, more frivolity.

Nothing's real, but nothing needs to be.

As Di drags me to the job fair; I wonder what the h*ll compelled me to bend to their wishes. I AM FUNDAMEN-TALLY OPPOSED TO THIS COMPANY. What's stopping me from screaming NO?

When they wanted a tablet at ten: NO.

When they begged for direct uploads: Not until you're seventeen! (We settled on fifteen.)

You can't stop the world from getting to your kids. You can only hope you've armed them with enough compassion to get through.

We arrive in a conference room grand enough to host

a ball; promo-holograms offer us complimentary choco-late mist; Di is accosted by five of their closest friends. They crowd the cutest hologram for a Selfie.

Di always had more friends than me. Always. Then again, it's a new generation. Maybe kids are kinder these days.

The presentation is convincing, certainly. It reminds me of recruitment ads for the army. All "Do Your Part" this and "Find Your Future" that. I wish I could shut it off, but it's wired into everyone's Direct Downloads.

All I can do is wait.

Attractive footage promises a Garden of Eden for all future Fun Farmers, claims supported by high-production footage of meditation classes, massage rooms, and outdoor gardens. It looks more like a holiday than a job.

Even I am tempted to apply. The air on that island is clean. The factory windows are large. So are the beds.

The grass is green.

Furthermore, the hands-on labour might be a good expe-rience for Di. I often fret they spend too much time in virtual and not enough time in reality.

FUN FARM BRINGS OUT YOUR BEST!

YOU ARE USEFUL!

LET FUN FARM SHOW YOU HOW!

I look around. Few guardians bothered to show up. Most likely jumped at the prospect of getting their kids away, all expenses paid, even if only for the summer.

Finally, the PSA's finished. As the images fade from our brains, I realize I was enchanted like everyone else but have managed to break the spell.

It's bullsh*t factory work that should have stayed in the 21st century. So what if there's medical benefits and sleeping quarters, plus a pension, and woodland grounds where you can walk and see real birds and smell real flowers and . . .

Everyone is ready to sign up, and most everyone does.

I swipe through the brochures, scan the leaflets, bide my time and slowly kill it, all the while hawk-eyeing little Di who, like all the other kids, has happily drained the Kool-Aid. They and several of their friends disappear into the Chill/VR Room; I pretend to read.

Crowds fade. Kids sign up and drift away. I thank f*ck for the VR Room, otherwise Di would be pestering me for permission.

"Here to sign up?" says a silky-smooth voice, the kind that makes you tingle before you even know who it is.

I'm not very visual, but this guy is gorgeous. He's so deep in the uncanny valley of handsomeness, I'm surprised by the pulse in his hands, hands he offers to me like they're the shirt off his back, and I'm a mugged man abandoned on the road.

"You're Di's guardian, correct? Lovely girl. I can see she comes by that honestly."

I take my hands away as politely as possible.

"Di is a they."

"My apologies! No offence intended." His eyes could melt an ice queen. "I spoke directly with Di prior to our presentation. *They* implied you may have misgivings regarding their potential employment with Fun Farm. You're a psychologist, yes?"

"I didn't catch your name."

He bows in a way that makes my head race—or is that my heart?

"Sona, at your service. Head Recruiter for Fun Farm Inc."

"Pleasure."

"And you are?"

"A concerned parent. I'm not so keen on my youngling being shipped off to an island I can't even visit."

"But you most certainly can! Visitors are welcome the

last weekend of every second month—or workers have the option to return to shore."

He is convinced he can convince me. I am convinced to remain unconvinced.

"I'd rather see it in person."

"Was the virtual tour not enough?"

I repeat, steelier this time, "I'd rather see it in person."

His smile remains. "I see that you care deeply for Di."

"I do."

"This is a wonderful opportunity for them. They clearly want to go."

"Di wants a lot of things. It's my job to temper their impulses."

"Oughn't we let the young ones follow their hearts?"

"There's a difference between self-direction and self-discipline. Discipline is what they require."

"Touché! Though I guarantee at Fun Farm they will find both." His smile has spread somewhere North of friendly, but then I remember where I lie on the sexy scale next to him. His charm could only be professional.

Di, ever the eavesdropper, pokes my elbow with their phone.

"Pleeeeease, sib! If I sign up today, we get an extra bonus: 500 bit, asap deposit!"

"Is that true?"

Sona confirms with the sexiest nod. (How can a nod be sexy? Ugh!)

We could really use the money. Most of my earnings from Sel go straight to paying off the debts my parents left, as hand workers in their time were paid a pittance, if that.

I look at Di. Their precious eyes pool with desire. I think of all the things I've had to deny them, all the things I've wanted to give.

Perhaps we can't protect anyone.

Perhaps we can only set them free.

"Is this really what you want?"

"Auto-totes! Pleeeeease. All my friends are going." Di's friends produce their stamped applications on their phones as evidence.

Everyone's waiting for me to give in, and of course, I do.

I have become the worst type of guardian: a hypocrite.

We leave hand in hand. I can't remember the last time Di let us link arms.

"Thanks, sib. Mega-thanks."

I don't know what to say except, "You'll text every day, yes?"

"Le duh. All the Fun Farmers are always texting back home. Cat's femme-sib went to the Farm two weeks ago, and they're always messaging: Love you. All's well. Sentimental cr*p like that.

That ain't me. I'ma waste all my text credits with the cr*ppiest cr*p. So many swears, all you'll hear is landmines! F*ck, f*ck, f*******ck!"

They bleep-bleep-bleep all the way home.

We laugh like we haven't in years.

I do love my little sibling. Sometimes, it's like they speak another language, but it turns out you don't need to speak the same way to understand someone.

Di texts me from the ferry:

*Miss you, sib. You're all my parental units racked up in one. F*ckity f*ck f*ck, etc!!!*

They can't send Snaps or Doodlez or Tix from the island. Fine by me; snaps drive me crazy.

I worry I've made a mistake but would probably worry equally if I forced them to stay home. They're nearly graduated and, unlike me, have a penchant for the popular and pertinent.

Kids like money. We need money. Why not let Di make

some?

But Mom and Dad . . .

UGH!

Why can't there be an app to censor THAT?

It's foolish to dwell on the past and fill your brain with What Ifs. Yet, some days are reserved for ruminating.

Our parents were some of the last of the hand working class: father a teacher, mother a doctor. Remember the picketers protesting screen laws? My dad was at the head of the pack. Mom couldn't march, busy as she was with all the cardiac arrests. We always joked Dad would be Mom's next patient if he didn't give himself a break.

Then one day, it wasn't funny anymore.

She followed him soon after, which I guess is typical when people are really in love. They left me at sixteen to take care of my little sib. I did the best I could, but even a decade later, I'm still trying to figure out what to do.

When religion was still in its dying days, a kid at school always said, "WWJD." I prefer What Would Mom And Dad Do.

"I just want what's best for Di."

"And you did the best you could." Sel dusts off a copy of Cicero so old, it should be illegal. For every book, I hand her a fresh rag. That's my job, apart from looking pretty, which I'm failing at today. "You made a choice which precipitated an action. Why worry?"

"What if they're miserable these next three months? What if they get sunburn? Those windows may not have enough UV blockers. Or arthritis? They rarely use their hands! They only ever type with their eyes!"

I collapse, and not in a good way.

Sel rubs my shoulders.

"One needn't regret anything unless one acts against their intuition."

"Which I did."

"*C'est la vie!* May as well let go."

"What if I screw everything up?" I let her turn me around. "What if I'm never going to be the kind of parent Di needs?"

She takes my lips on her own.

"You worry too much."

I'm starting to think I worry just the right amount.

SAD?

MAD?

SCARED?

NO FEAR—FUN FARM IS HERE!

DON'T GET LEFT BEHIND!

ONE CLICK AND IT'S ALL GOOD TIMES!

DON'T DELAY!

DOWNLOAD FUN FARM TODAY!

I'm too pissed off to swear.

Every morning, I wake to temptation, fresh and ripe, but can't dare pluck such sexy, forbidding fruit. Call it pride. Call it cowardice. I am simply too stubborn to join the pack.

Or maybe I'm scared of being happy.

I lie in bed a little too long. Sel lets me take weekends off, and with Di gone, there's no reason to get up.

Nothing to do but wait for their good morning text.

Sure enough:

Good morning!

Those lonely, faceless letters across my eyes is almost

enough to bring me back to life.

Hey, I type back with my fingers, which according to Di makes me a dinosaur. *Miss you. Everything okay?*

Luv you! All's well.

It takes a minute to register this is an oncoming text from my little sibling, one who forgoes empty platitudes.

I am in such a rush to type back, I succumb to insta-text instead of the keyboard:

Whatttt? oYu oky?

The reply is immediate:

No worries! It's great here. All's well.

Why didn't they make fun of my typos?

Di?

Yes?

What's wrong you with?

Nothing. I'm happy. 😄

I stare at that emoji for a long, long time.

Di hates emojis.

WWMADD?

For once, I know the answer.

They'd do anything to make sure Di was okay.

I've got to join the Fun Farm.

I stare at the number Sona plugged in to my phone "just in case." Is this the calling card to my damnation, or Di's salvation?

F*ck it.

I phone him.

He's a little less handsome as a projection (the filters are always creepy), but I'm disarmed all the same.

"Sona!"

When he sees it's me, he puts on his nicest mask.

"What a pleasure!"

"When's the next wave of workers heading out? Can you

get me in? I know it's last minute . . ."

"Terribly sorry. All applications are closed atm. The Factory is full."

D*MMIT.

"But I've got to get in!"

Is that a smirk I see?

"You've changed your tune. Psychology not paying well?"

"It never did. That's not my worry."

"What could you possibly be worried about?"

There's so much I need to say; none of it can be said online.

"Can you get downtown? Meet me at the park? Fifty secs?"

"The park?" he sheds his salesman vibe like a heavy coat. "What are we, squirrels?"

"You liked Di, didn't you?"

"I liked how she upped my commission."

"Please!"

Siiiiiiigh.

"Fine."

As he predicted and I hoped, we're the only humans here. This park's a farce of nature but grants solace all the same. The grass is fake, but the trees are real, and that's enough for me.

I trace my hand across a tree's bark to avoid looking at Sona; he's even prettier than I remembered.

"Is this a date?" he wonders.

"That's the last thing I'm thinking about!" (Okay, the second, but the first sure as h*ll takes precedent.)

"Then what are we doing here? Do you want money? 'Cause I'm not giving you any. I'm a recruiter, not a charity."

"I need you to get me into the Farm."

"I already told you," he says on his way out, "applications are closed."

"Please! It's for Di."

Something like a conscience blocks his exit. Without turning around, he guesses,

"You miss her?"

"Worse."

I hurriedly sum up my concerns, finishing with what I hope is a powerful rendition of the foreboding emoji story.

He can't understand why an emoji should evoke such consternation.

"Have you even been to the Fun Farm? Who knows what they're doing to them out there!"

"Why do you even care?"

"Why don't you?"

"I'm not paid to!"

"No, you're paid to coax the slaves onto the ship."

"That's a little hyperbolic, don't you think?"

"This coming from the man who sets his smile filter to stun every morning!"

"You know *nothing* about me."

True. TBH, I wasn't thinking of him as anything more than a way in, or a way through. But he is a person, in-person. One I can actually talk to.

Sel is wonderful, in her way, but it's not the same as being somewhere just because I want to be.

Or being with someone I want to be with.

Aren't psychologists supposed to help people? Connect with them?

When did I leave my dreams behind?

"I'm sorry. There's no reason to lash out at you. I mean, you met me here. You didn't have to."

Sona brushes it off, but I can tell he's just as lonely as me, if not more so. He has to show up every day, condemned to the sparkling lies. I have the luxury of hiding. As does Sel.

As for Di, their life was all fun and games until they went away and misplaced their personality.

"You can lie all you want, but I know you liked Di. And I know you like me."

His scoff is suspect.

I wonder if psychologists are better at manipulating people than helping them.

I'm too honest to take advantage.

"I'm scared, okay? Di is the one person in this world who really matters to me. I shouldn't have let them go away. And I'm prepared to do anything to right that mistake."

He turns around, hesitates. I try one more time.

"Pleeeeease?"

I've channeled Di. He smiles a real-life smile, tries to recover with a head shake, but it's too late. We've both gotten under his skin.

"C'mon, give me a try."

I don't consider how sexy that sounds until his hands are on my waist, and my hands are in his hair, and his eyes are on my eyes in a way nobody's looked at me in my life—or if they did, I didn't care.

We enter a kiss that may lighten our burdens, if only for a moment.

Or six.

I didn't expect to have sex with him—least of all for free. I guess I've sold myself for a ticket to Paradise (or Purgatory). But as I've known for a while with Sel, these arrangements are always complicated.

He plays with my hair. I play with his.

"So?" I kiss him once more for good measure. "Will you be my Trojan stud? Get me in?"

He kisses me back, for old time's sake.

"What can I even do?"

"You can make me look good! That's what you're good at, right?"

Sigh. I'm surprised he can breathe out that long.

"Fine."

He says he'll "do what he can," which means very little, but it's all I have. He encourages me to keep an eye out for listings in the management department. As soon as I see one, I pounce and am delighted to get an interview asap.

Looks like Sona's influence is stronger than he anticipated.

As always with these online jobs, the interviewer knows much more about me than I'd like.

"You're a book writer, aren't you?" she asks, eyes shiny and glazed from the screen filter.

THAT'S a stumbling point. Books are a pariah, blamed for corrupting the youth far more than drugs.

"I mean, I wrote *a* book, singular."

"Yes, *On the Eradication of the Psyche*. Fascinating work. Exactly what we want to see in a Fun Farm employee."

"Seriously?"

For once, I'm glad eye contact is becoming obsolete.

"We're told you wrote the book *with your hands*. Is that true?"

"Well, I typed it."

"But with your *hands*?"

"Yes."

"Fascinating! When can you start?"

This is too easy!

"If I may be so bold, my philosophies appear to run rampant against your own."

"That's precisely why we want you."

Her smile makes me sick. Come to think of it, she's probably AI.

Click! She exits, and I'm left somewhere between terror and elation.

I'm in!

Sel takes the rejection well, all things considered.

"Am I not paying you enough?" she smiles, but behind her eyes lies an unmistakable pain, one no app could relieve.

Like me, she must suffer wholly.

"This way, I can work from home. I'm doing stuff with user interface. User feedback. User everything."

"That doesn't sound like you."

"It's not," I admit. "But for now, it's necessary."

She unpacks a brand-new book.

"This is about losing Di, isn't it?"

I don't have to say a thing. She always sees right through me.

After a parting tryst, I watch her in bed while she meditates, all the while puffing on her delicious cigarette. I know this is my cue but take my time. I'll miss her, with all her easy wisdom and loud laughter and old books.

Before I leave, she opens one eye and delivers a goodbye that's a lot more like an omen.

"If you must tread those waters, do so lightly.

And if you must dive deep, be sure to come up for air."

We kiss, and though I've kissed her many times swearing I'd never come back, this one really feels like the last.

Sona does help me look good. He CC's me on all the right emails, and I soon find myself sneaking up the corporate ladder, not a snake in sight.

Some of my success may be attributed to my own merit. Psychologists have become the unicorns of marketing. My shallow excursions of the human psyche are exactly what they require to guarantee Fun Farm's position as the most in-demand (read: addictive) app in existence.

I don't know why they're worried; the app sells itself. Every day, its stock goes up, and after an emotional eternity (i.e, two and a half months), there's another call for factory workers, which means another ferry off to the island, and a ferry I will be on, or die trying to board.

I relay my intentions to Sona as I lie in his arms, and he in mine.

"Nobody in management has ever traveled to the factory."

"Then you and I will be the first."

It's a relief to have a fellow conspirator—especially one I can kiss.

Everything's alright—or it will be, when I see Di again.

Their daily texts only fill me with dread:

Hi! How's it going?

All's well.

Luv you!

These updates plague me for all their absence of Di's individuality. I'm probably the only guardian who worries.

I'm probably the only guardian who texts their kid.

Di and I have a complicated relationship. Always did. How could we not? I was one part mother, one part sister; they my lifeline *and* my ball-and-chain. Ever since they left, I've been adrift, with only Sona to ground me, and even then, the relief is ever temporary.

My fear still swirls, my rage burns on, and though Sona advises me to try Fun Farm "just once," I know it won't help.

All that matters is getting Di home. They need me, but I'm coming to realize I need them even more.

I only took Psychology because of my mood disorder. I wanted to understand myself and, by extension, better understand others.

I've never avoided Fun Farm on principle. That's what I'd like people to believe, but the truth is far more selfish and simple.

I'm afraid it won't work.

Apps are designed for the neurotypical, not those of us who regularly crash in and out of brutal emotional swings.

I've braved my lot in life so far; no point moaning now. Just because I dip so, so low or rage so, so hard doesn't mean

I fail to appreciate the simpler pleasures of these synapses, like humour and hope, comfort or joy. I may even appreciate them more! Indeed, I am blessed by these valleys, for only through them can I ascend to the peaks, peaks which for many can only be accessed via a monthly subscription.

We are only a slave to our minds. I am free.

As it turns out, the only employees exempted from the no-island rule are high-ranking recruiters and . . . psychologists.

The powers-that-be allowed Sona a tour of the grounds, and he greased their wheels long enough to permit a plus-one.

The ferry leaves at 10AM, arriving at the Fun Farm by 1015. This leaves fifteen entire minutes of watching the sky meet the sea, like something out of a storybook.

The new recruits gather in gaggles on deck, reminding me far too much of Di and their friends. I distract myself with that unparalleled vision of a blue horizon.

If I didn't know better, I'd call it beautiful.

In ten minutes, land is ahoy. The island appears first as a shadow interrupting the skyline and soon emerges as a vision in its own right: far mountains and rolling hills, serene and picturesque.

The grass is real. The sky is clear.

There might even be birdsong.

The factory is huge and daunting, but lovely in its own way, and only a five-second air-train from shore. It boasts the same huge windows as proclaimed in the PSA. I half-hope I'll see Di humming away on an assembly line. The factory has many floors, all filled with offices and sexy AI workers in tight, sexy suits and tight, sexy skirts.

There's not a Fun Farmer anywhere.

At least, nowhere near the windows.

We flash our passes at the scary security guard who is clearly disinterested, except perhaps in checking us out. We must look good in our business formal and matching sunglasses—almost good enough to be AIs.

Nobody is suspicious, as far as we can see. Why should they be?

We play hide-and-seek, hiding from potential onlookers and seeking Di. The new recruits were taken off-ship first, and we haven't seen them since we landed.

It's hard to believe that, in the midst of this breathtaking scenery (I even see a butterfly!), Di might be suffering nearby.

Inspired by our mission and my fervour, Sona has grown in confidence, and before we left charmed his way into the factory's blueprints. We don't know much, but we know there's a back entrance.

Before we go in, we kiss.

Why does it feel like our last?

The best life is on the other side of risk.

That's what my professor always said.

Granted, she was an amalgamated consciousness of many old, dead philosophers/psychologists, but I like to think I learned a lot from her and that much of what she said was true, or close to it.

If the best life is on the other side of risk, then the best feeling is on the other side of fear, and right now, fear is all I know.

I don't know what I'm more afraid of: finding Di, or not finding Di.

Indoors reminds me too much of home. I'd rather be outside.

This is not the sort of place one goes running around in, but then again, it's not the sort of place that should ever fear a security breach. We may in fact find more than we intend.

I don't know what I'm looking for, save for Di, but I know secrets are best kept in basements, so that's where we go.

The deeper we go, the darker it gets, and a hum that was

once white-noise nuisance becomes all-enveloping.

Hall upon hall, door after door—all unlocked, mostly leading to nothing, which seems more suspicious than anything else.

Sel always told me to trust my intuition. Some knot near my clit screams STOP. So, I stop.

To my right is a door we missed, a door essentially part of the wall, with no handle, no hinges, hardly even a visible crack, marked only by a modest binary plaque:

01110100 01101000 01100101 00100000 01100110
01100001 01110010 01101101

Sona translates:

"The Farm."

It's a deep room, deeper than it is tall, but tall all the same, the only light a sad glow from blue screens attached to gurneys.

Row upon row of disparate youth lie on their bellies as if on massage beds, with the same hole for their head you'd expect, only what should be a cushion is a mass of wires and plugs, worse than any crown of thorns.

Row upon row of tortured souls sob, blubber, wail and writhe, screams made all the worse by the silence. Their faces are the only indication of their peril, and it is acute.

I dare to examine the screen in one of their heads. It's exactly as I feared:

RAD TO MAD!

CHEER TO FEAR!

ECSTASY TO AGONY!

Bad feelings don't just disappear. They have to go somewhere.

You can't bypass suffering. You can only pass it on.

"Of course. It's a trade."

I laugh. It's one sullen, searing bark and cuts across the all-too-quiet room.

"Trade your Sad for Glad. Take someone else's gladness, and they get your sorrow instead. A perfect arrangement. Except for the ones on this end."

Sona's hand covers his perfect teeth and perfect lips. I doubt he'll be seeking new recruits anytime soon.

I should have known it would come to this.

It's all a matter of desire.

Everyone wants the burger, and no one need meet the cow.

I want to smash this place up. Bleed the neck of every f*cker who pays to get their pain taken away. Flay the genius rich who funded this project and make millions as these sad souls sob next to me, disallowed from even making a sound.

That's when I see them: third row down, three from the left, so close I can almost touch them.

I'd know them anywhere. Any crowd. Any time.

Di.

I run to their side and know they're not done yet. They are one of the most resilient brats I know. They can't be broken.

Not yet.

I can't bear to look at their face and look instead to Sona, who is far more fluent in technology.

He disconnects Di with ease. The machines must need to be changed out quick when the farmers give out. I shudder to think what happens to them then.

Finally free, Di falls into our arms. Their tortured face turns neutral; they are out of agony and back in the room.

When they know for sure it's me and I'm not some cruel hallucination, they crash against me and cry.

We don't have much time.

"Sona! Your phone-filter. Quick!"

Before he can comply, I take it from him and wash Di's neon fringe with brown locks as boring as my own.

"What are you . . . ?"

"Nobody took a good look at me when I came in. With my clothes and my pass, Di will be a suitable replacement. And I'll be a fine replacement for them."

Sans ceremony, I strip and bid Di trade me her ugly zippered one-piece.

"No!" Sona cries, looking almost as disturbed as Di.

"C'mon, Sona. Help me out. Plug me in."

"Don't make me do this!" begs Sona.

"You have to come with us!" begs Di.

"We can't all leave! If they find one of the farmers missing, they'll catch us before we cross water. You two need to get off the island without incident."

Di can't stop crying, and I know those tears are all their own. I look deep inside their sweet, kind eyes and manage a smile.

"I'll be fine. It can't be any worse than one of my bad days."

A lie, of course, but it's truer for me than most. I've never run away from the worst emotions, and I'm not about to start now.

Di submits to playing dress-up, like we did back when Mom and Dad were alive, when we were a family, and maybe even happy. We're so close to the same size, it's an easy switch. I zip up the ugly one-piece; it sucks on my skin from Di's terrified, tortured sweat.

I lie on the free station and stick my face through the hole.

"We'll be back for you." Sona almost makes it sound like a promise. "We'll be back for everyone! We'll get you all out of here."

I don't know whether to laugh or cry but figure one of the app's users will soon decide that for me.

My nod to Sona: consent to lock me in. Di reaches for my hand, but I can't hold anything once I'm plugged in.

The wires whir. My temple pulses. The room begins to fade.

"Go! Go! It's okay."

It's all going to be okay.

Hell is soon to start. Too many log in to rid themselves of loneliness, heartache, boredom, misery, terror, rage.

If only they knew who shoulders the burden for them.

How ironic that, as I wait to be stuffed with other people's peril, I am totally at ease. For the first time in a while, there's no anger, no loss, no regret, no need. All that lifted off as I watched Di and Sona slip away, Di a spitting doppelganger of me, and I knew they'd get home, and stay safe.

I'm at peace knowing the world goes on, and that I contributed a piece.

The End

Fly, My Pretty

M Y NEW PIMP'S ACROSS the street.
I don't know how I can see him when I'm on the third floor, and I don't know how I know it's him when I've never seen him before, but he is clear in my mind as crystal; I can tell from the strut.

Soon, he'll be up the stairs, through the door, and I tell myself, "You don't have to do this. You can leave whenever you want."

I see the balcony through those big, glass patio doors, and I run and jump! But I know I'll never fall.

I catch the undercurrent. SWOOP! And flap of arms.

I am over the buildings and everywhere.

I forgot how good it felt to fly! Dead memories rush back to life: nights and days wind flattered my face, as free as anyone could be.

I soar. I smile.

Soon, I am higher than clouds.

Up here, it's only birds and me.

I know I can't keep the peak, so I dip to caress the tips of trees. I decide to follow the left road; it looks dangerous, beautiful. The wind has other plans. Once I veer West, she knocks me back, a gulping, gushing gust. I grab a branch; it snaps.

"Okay: I'll trust the wind."

LEAP! The wind lifts me like a babe, rushes me East.

For a moment, I think I'm even higher than before. Clouds cover me in swarms, but this is fog. I should have known when the hawks didn't follow.

The fog opens for reckless rocks jutting from the ocean.

Fear is for those who aren't brave enough to fly.

I screech, duck, and dive. The waves crash, but the rocks sinkb and blue stretches above and below.

Now, there is nothing but me.

I've never been this far out to sea. The sun falls, the moon rises to tuck it to sleep, and I learn the ocean is alive and angry. Waves turn to mouths with huge throats and bigger teethb and they snap, snap, snap; I curl my toes, suck my breath, and reach.

Even this close to death, I laugh.

The moon falls. The ocean melts. I'm neither falling nor flying; now, it's somersaults through space. When I roll right-side-up, I'm in a hot spring, and strange, yellow smiles surround me like the t-shirts that say, "Have a nice day," and they speak with bubbles above their heads like those comic books I bought from drugstores as a kid and they say, "Who's this?" and, "You're an ace!"

I wonder where my wings went because I am armless. I think, "Is this the future?" and I'm terrified.

A smile separates from the crowd. They look soft, and they have arms, and they're reaching out to me, and my own arms grow back because I'm dying for intimacy.

Freedom's fine, but nothing beats being held.

I submit to a deep, dark hug, one that swallows, forgives, and protects.

I forgot how much I loved this.

The hot spring cools. The smiles disappear.

My new pimp holds me under his head. I am soothed by the rhythm of his chest. I don't know how I know him, but I think I always did; I don't know how I can be everywhere at once or how freedom is a feeling in my mouth, folded in my wings, tucked under my belt, and that's why I'm never afraid.

"Where'd you get to?" he says. "I came upstairs, and you were gone!"

The End

This Happened №1

HE PARKS HIS EL Camino between the daycare and crema-
torium in the hopes to see his kid.

Nobody knows where the ex lives. Nobody's even sure if
there's a kid. Yet, he parks, waits, sits. Every. Damn. Morning.

There's something depressingly sexy about a 30-some-
thing running out of cigs for a glimpse of what may not be
his.

Spoiler: it ain't.

Either way, he waits, which is why it was quite a fuck-me
day when he asked me to meet him at the shitty diner on 74th
St where the waitress is twelve years old and six feet tall.

He kept his sunglasses on. When he finally took them
off, I could see why: his usually brilliant green eyes were re-
duced to muggy seaweed.

He would not. Stop. Blinking.

"Coffee?" asked the smiling server who thankfully was
not the hot twelve-year-old.

"Not for me," I said, broke af.

"Do you have grapefruit juice?" he asked.

"I'll have the same!"

He is the only coke dealer I know who likes grapefruit juice.

The waitress brought us our grapefruit "cocktails" (yuck); my friend ordered the Cowboy Breakfast with a side of pancakes.

What he said next was even more shocking than his source in Croatia getting busted.

"The ex rang."

"The ex?"

"Yep."

"YOUR ex?"

"Yep."

"On a telephone?"

"Yep."

"You have a telephone. And your ex called you on it."

"Yes and yes."

"Holy shit. I didn't think she existed."

"Just barely."

His pancakes came cold; he didn't notice. Nor did he notice when I slipped one off the plate.

"She was freaked. Went to pick up her mom from the hospital, and there was some black guy . . ."

(He didn't say "black guy," by the way.)

". . . fucking harassing them. She was crying. She was freaked. I mean, think of this: her mom's in a goddamn wheelchair, and there's some freak pulling out his dick and waving it in their fucking faces . . ."

"Why didn't they get the police?"

"What planet are you from?"

Fair enough.

"So, I went to pick them up, dropped them off at my place. Then I circled back to look for this creep.

I saw him in the parking lot and told him just what I thought about guys who whip out their dicks on old ladies.

He took his dick out on ME, called me a f*****, and I'm

like . . ." His eyes rolled to the back of his head, and I pretty much got the gist.

"So, I got out my retractable axe."

Uh oh.

"Drove around to find him. Came up from behind and . . . you know, people never tell you about the LITTLE things. Like how all this blood gets on your pants or the CRACK when something hits a skull. He went DOWN, and I knew he was dead, like knew for sure I just killed a man. And I left him gurgling, and my first thought was I gotta get to the ex . . ."

"Good god man, don't go ruining your life over a girl."

"You say that to everybody."

"It's good advice." I took his last pancake. "What happened next?"

"Silly bitch called the police. She didn't know what I'd done. When I didn't come back, she got freaked, and then I came back bathed in blood and, well . . . I may have to get out of the city."

He rambled on about Croatia and Cuba and Anywhere-But-Here, but we both knew he was talking shit.

Nobody gets out of this city. It holds on, sucks you in, and doesn't even spit you out after you're dead.

Yet he spoke so fervently of escape, I wanted to believe it was possible. Imagine if we could all be free. How would freedom feel?

"It's nobody's fault that we're fucked. That's how it is everywhere. Mash a bunch of people together, and the same shit always happens. Blood and guts and bullshit."

"Uh, how's the food?" asked a trepidatious waitress.

"Great," I lied.

"Are you listening to us?" asked my sweet, sad friend, eyes all the more buggy.

It's a shame when he gets paranoid/violent, because he really is lovely. He has beautiful arms with beautiful tattoos on them and, once upon a time, had beautiful cats and a beautiful TV before all the technology was smashed to bits.

I remember when we used to sit on his porch, drink raspberry lemonade, and talk about our feelings like they were important.

Back when life was for the living.

"No, sir, I . . ."

"You're recording this, aren't you?" he threw his sunglasses at her head, which was probably excessive. He proceeded to call her every epithet under the moon, which was definitely excessive, and I know I should have said something in allyship but was too busy shoveling back the rest of his breakfast.

Morals are easier to enforce after you're fed.

I'm sorry to say he grabbed the waitress by the throat, and by that point, I thought it necessary to step in, but my poor, sweet friend was in too deep to back down.

"I'll burn this whole fuckin place down! I got NOTHING to lose now!"

Nobody wanted to deal with this. Nobody was going to call the police on a handsome white man in the midst of a nervous breakdown. They wanted us to GTFO ASAP, and with good reason.

I very politely asked for the bill, which was very politely left on our table.

I don't really know what I said to calm him down. I probably told a lot of lies to make him feel better about life, and he eventually let go of that poor old sister's throat and dropped money on the table for the shitty food/outstanding customer service.

"Is that a good tip? 6 bucks on an $18 bill?"

"That's a GREAT tip, dood."

"Good."

The End

The Power of Pepper Spray

THE BIG CITY IN June is perfection. People walk their dogs, even in Needle Park. The dogs come in all colours, shapes, and sizes, as do the people. Millennials cramp their legs on grass, let worms ruin their picnics, and complain. Old folks take their time and complain a little less. White people burn. Chinese women protect themselves under parasols. BFs snap pics of their GFs, and so do BFFs, or BFFN (Best Friends For Now).

Moreover, there is seldom a cloud in the sky, and when there is, it appears so benign, you could blow it away like one blows out a birthday candle.

At least, this was all true the summer Akshita decided to die.

Akshita was not conventionally pretty but incredibly sexy. Her breasts and eyes were too small by North American beauty standards, but anyone who met her mouth found infinite pleasure within, the sort of bliss you will inevitably regret and never be able to forget.

She was a Venus relegated to earthly dimensions thirty-three years prior. Few Venuses were sent to Earth since the Marilyn Monroe debacle, and the Venuses decided they'd better do something about that.

They sent Akshita to Earth so humans could teach her love.

Alas, this girl could never love herself enough to love anyone else. She was a fine whore and a good friend but never exceptional, for love is the root of all things, and love is ever false until turned inward.

A Venus cannot properly give love until she receives it. This is the first rule of the Venuses and the first Akshita broke.

Love looked easy on everyone else. She studied humans with their pets (especially dogs). When couples held hands, she took notes (particularly if they were happy, or old, or both). Yet, the idea of loving oneself without touching oneself seemed remiss, and no matter how hard she tried, saying, "I Love You" to the mirror remained a lie.

This is why she thought it best to die.

On her way to the bridge (for she thought death-by-jumping most romantic), a trick chirped from his 1957 Pontiac Bonneville:

"Hey sister, you working?"

"Who talks like that?" she wondered.

"I've got business for you."

Akshita never kept her head down when harassed. She always kept it high—so high, she sometimes tripped.

"No funny business," he promised. "Just business."

Akshita would usually reject the invite of a trailing car driven by a black man in a bowler hat, but she figured, "What the hell—one for the road," and climbed in.

"There's a graveyard near here. Pretty discreet."

"I told you. No funny business. Just business."

She took a better look at the backseat: typewriter (broken and robin-egg blue, like the car), blanket, canned beans.

Then she took a better look at the man.

His eyes were small like hers, and like her, he was not

exceptionally pretty but symmetrical and very sexy. He had soft, small hands; he looked shy and screamed post-grad.

This was not the sort of John you'd expect from a corner pick-up.

He parked, reached for the glove compartment, and calmly revealed a straight razor.

Akshita calmly whipped out her pepper spray.

"Glad to see you brought it." Further shuffling produced a shaving brush and cream. "Now, do forgive me while I run from my 5 o'clock shadow."

He proceeded to shave, rearview mirror his humble vanity.

"Now." He spread what looked like whipped cream all over his chin "First to confirm, you are indeed Akshita, daughter of Venus?"

Akshita kept her pepper spray ready.

"Excuse me?"

"No need to play coy. We Venuses must stick together, no?"

"You're a ... ?"

"Isn't it obvious?"

"Frankly, no."

The man laughed.

"Fine, maybe I'm not July in the calendar spread, but I'm at least a June. As a matter of fact, that's my name. Pleased to meet you."

"I wish I could say the same, June. But I'm pretty sore on Venuses at the moment."

"Yes, yes. We've been waiting for updates on your love lesson. Not faring well, is it?"

Akshita seriously considered slipping out of the car.

"Ironic," June continued. "A Venus not knowing how to love herself."

"It's none of your business." Akshita, among many things, was very private. "Surely, this isn't why you interrupted my busy schedule? To berate me on how bad I am at love?"

"To the contrary. I'm here to recruit you."

Right on cue, a lightning bolt shattered the windshield. Both ducked; tiny spots of glass spat themselves on skin.

"Your time and energy would be most appreciated . . . !"

ZING! What sounded like an arrow hit the side mirror. Bullseye.

"What the . . . ?"

"Keep your pepper spray close, my dear." June rolled out of the car, shave complete. "You're going to need it."

Akshita thought it odd he left the razor.

Five men were on the attack; June and Akshita were at a terrible disadvantage. At the point in a movie where villains and heroes exchange witty banter and/or ominous warnings, these men were on a full-frontal, forward assault, with an arsenal including but not limited to bow-and-arrows, iron knuckles, and apparently, lightning bolts.

June tapped the hood of the car; it flipped itself over like a dog showing off a trick, and behind this, the Venuses sought cover.

"I'm calling the police . . ." Akshita began, only to re-member some anti-technology activist broke her phone the week before.

"No need! I've been expecting these gentlemen. Though I will admit, I'm not much of a fighter. That's where you come in."

"What exactly gave you the impression I can help you with this?!" Akshita wanted to close her eyes and never open them again.

June looked deep into Akshita's eyes with such sincerity, Akshita had to listen.

"You know how to fight, Akshita. You've been fighting your whole life."

This was hardly enough to console her, but June offered nothing more.

Reluctant, she followed him into the fray.

There was something wrong about these men. For one thing, they were far too beautiful. Akshita had never seen anyone like them (on earth). If she dared eye contact, she would lose all track of where she was or what she was doing or why. This created another obvious advantage for the attackers.

They were all very tall, very white, and all ran at her, weapons ready.

It is folly to describe a fight, especially when five against two, and almost everyone is using magic of some kind. For Akshita, all was a blur, much like most of her first times. How could her hand turn into a fist that might have broken that man's nose? How could she duck that lightning bolt?

How could one tiny pack of pepper spray make these men to fall to their knees.

It was only later Akshita realized the power of these men was in their eyes. If she sprayed them, they could no longer fight, and their charms were altogether impotent.

Everyone was soon immobilized, thanks to one working girl and her pepper spray.

Her new friend June approached the first thug. She expected him to "finish the job" and was most surprised when he bent forward to kiss the man three times: once on either cheek and a final smack on the forehead.

POP-A-LOP-LOP!

Apparently, turning someone into a typewriter sounds a lot like popcorn.

Akshita dropped her pepper spray. The horribly handsome man transformed into a Sears typewriter from the 70s. He was a very pretty grey.

She watched in awkward awe as June continued to pop and flop all around until there was nobody but them.

"Cheers, sister. I couldn't have done it without you."

"I beg to differ." Akshita dared to poke the nearest

typewriter that had previously been an angry man. "What on earth ... ?"

"Seldom on earth, but often beyond it."

"What did you do to these men?!"

"First of all, they're hardly men. Second of all, it's a lot kinder than it looks." When Akshita remained unsatisfied, June conceded to elaborate. "I'm a freelancer, my dear. And I prefer to multitask. My primary initiative is to collect those in need of rehabilitation and take them to The Warehouse. My second is to recruit those in need of purpose."

"Where do you take them?"

"Who?"

"The ones who need a purpose."

"Wherever they need to go."

June returned Akshita's pepper spray, encouraging her fingers to close around it.

"You are long lost, my love. What's that song some humans sing? Looking for love in all the wrong places ..."

"I'm not a lover." Akshita finally realized this was true. "I'm a fighter. You said so yourself."

"The best lovers fight for all they love." June's smile was so sweet, Akshita had to return the favour.

June's Pontiac rolled over again, apparently without direction.

"Oh, my poor friend!" June petted the car. "We'll have you fixed up soon enough, promise. Oh, Akshita, do you mind ... ?" June indicated the small succession of typewriters: one pink, one blue, one grey, and one ancient, black Underwood.

One by one, they carried their complacent captives to the backseat.

"Job well done," June said, mostly to himself. He gave one of the villains a loving stroke on its keys. The typewriter replied with a surprisingly grateful ping.

"Is this what you're recruiting me for?" Akshita tried to

remember the last time she stayed with a man in a parked car this long without requiring a condom. "To help you lug around human typewriters?"

"Not everyone turns to typewriters, you know. We have about two rooms full of pinball machines. But I digress. You needn't help me with those who require rehabilitation."

June turned the key in the ignition. Akshita could have sworn she heard the car yawn. It was probably her imagination, but at this point, anything was possible.

"What I need is for you to recruit other recruiters."

"Like a . . . spiritual Ponzi Scheme?"

"Don't do yourself such disservice! I'm so busy with other collections, I'm lucky if I pick up one would-be hero on my way out of town. You, on the other hand, could make it your full-time gig. What say you?"

Akshita thought about it long and hard. She thought about the long nights that were always so lonely, no matter whom she was with. She thought about the First Nations reserves without clean drinking water; dogs beaten to death on country roads; girls and boys without homes; the misfits and fuckups and nobodies in dire need of a raison d'être.

". . . You can just drop me off at the bridge."

The End

First Date №2

*"That girl may seem like she's all tough
and over it, but she's fragile."*

—*Samantha,* Sex and the City

I DON'T KNOW ABOUT THESE awkward Human Moments. I.e.:

Your ex-boyfriend of two days is hitting on the chick your ex-bandmate brought to the gig, and the guy who's letting you crash for another week 'cause you have no cash 'til October 13th plays ambient piano, his fingers like sleepy spiders; and you know you're writing all this to distract yourself from the cortisol crashing through your chest, or maybe it's your heart because HE DOESN'T CARE about you. He's doing it AGAIN, the only difference is, this time, you finally dumped him.

You shouldn't care, but you do, so you breathe, for This Too Shall Pass.

Who cares how many twenty-four-year-olds he wants to do MDMA with? Just go, go dance, fake a smile, lie for one more night. One more night, and you'll be free, but why not be free now?

I do not want to hate anyone; maybe everyone needs a little hate. He ALWAYS pulled this shit, especially when he drank tequila.

Who cares, move on, forgive.

Few people hurt others on purpose. Most jerks are simply ignorant. Often when you think, "What a jerk," it's a miscommunication. It's far harder to humanize someone when you can't understand them. Therein lies little rifts of loss and hurt and jealousy, i.e. the reason you left your ex's birthday party early just in time to see some guy pee in the bushes.

I have to admire the daring of drunks/the homeless. I have to hope I'll rock this loser/failure complex and tomorrow will be a bit better.

Except I'm scared he'll never grow up. He'll always manifest new hookups, new first dates, new girls to introduce to drugs. And I'll get older and smarter, and he won't do either, and what if that hurts so much, I can't even be his friend?

The End

Forget About Me

MY WHOLE LIFE, I never craved the saviour, but the instigator.

"Leave her alone. I said leave her alone!"

"You gonna make me?"

"Yeah."

I finger myself against my panties.

Do all (hetero) girls go for bad boys? Are we trained to get off on disrespect? Whatever do my kinks mean for the (first wave) feminist movement?

How can I be sex-positive when everything makes me feel like shit?

I finger my loaned-out ashtray, while on-screen, *The Breakfast Club* continues its teen-addled melodrama.

My eyes are looking out for the magic.

There's too much media. Above, I hear neddy techno-grub; beneath me are moans of a lonely pornographic soundtrack.

My basement neighbour's getting off on watersport clips. Not that I'm one to judge, combing my clit to memories of narcissistic ex-boyfriends, narcissistic one-night stands, narcissistic, etc.

My fingers push my pulsing cherry-top, but I can't get off, not with all these noises and headaches and praying my baby won't wake up.

The upstairs couple is smashing bottles again.

Rage-phrases crack the bass, rocketing shards of "bitch," "cheating," "liar," and "jerk" to pop ecstasy tabs of their own.

All those two do is fight.

If only they had better taste in music.

My hand stalls, wetness caked and going cold.

What does love mean, anyway? Does it all boil down to "bitch" and "jerk" and little glass kiss-cuts?

I wonder what they do when the fever stops and they have to sweep up.

No wonder they keep the gangster rap cranked. White noise offers respite from awkward silences.

Below, a certain someone's ready for his closeup. His sweaty self-love grunts are antithetical to my own arousal.

"Hunh . . . fff . . . mmm . . ."

His is the symphony of loneliness.

My therapy group suggested a bubble bath, soothing music, warming lubricants—anything to soak the sponge of desire. One girl returned to her very first fantasy. All this mess of digging up your sexual roots. I think she called it, "liberating."

"Being bad feels pretty good, huh?"

This isn't working.

"Hmh! . . ." One apartment under, this cry comes as a false spike, a peak that never was, a misleading wad of pre. I can picture the hunched beer belly, wiggling paunch, contorted, dismal face. A face that should be warped with pleasure but instead comes out agonized.

What secrets does that expression hide?

I wince, rewind.

"Over the bra, under the blouse, shoes off, hoping to God . . ."

"DON'T TOUCH ME!" comes the upstairs commentary from a voice so abject and shrill, I can't determine the gender.

Fast forward.

So crowded, so alone. My skirt and socks are still on, but my soul's stripped, bruise-wrapped and belly-up in a snow trench.

So what if I'm fucked about sex? I can still have a good time in the midst of my quarter-life crisis.

Freud was wrong. I attended enough of Intro to Psych to know that.

From above the ceiling: *Untsauntsauntsawrreeeee*

Can that really be considered music?

Coupled with, "GO TO HELL!" and followed by a cornucopia of onomatopoeias: smash, crinkle, stomp, and a SMACK which I can only assume means someone got slapped.

From below the carpet: "Nnnnnngh!"

And a burst of finality: "Whoo!"

At least someone's puncturing nirvana tonight.

I give up, wash my hands of pleasure.

My little girl has her tiny hands closed into pretty fists. She looks happy in her sleep.

This body remains a vacant space. This body only makes sense to me if someone else uses it for their own gains.

Meanwhile, girls stay with boys who say all the right dirty words when they're not playing Grover Alexander to a jug of Jack (Or re-enacting Mike Tyson on your face).

Companionship is a basic human instinct. What do we have left if we deny ourselves sweet toxicity? Piss porn. *The Breakfast Club*. Hands getting tired and old.

For a long time, I sought out people "like me." Some were kind, some were creeps. All felt a deep affinity with pain.

My hand wanders back to my leaking inkwell. The drips are stale. My fingers stick. I sit down again, screen flickering in the almost-midnight gloom as I explore my Pandora's box, one that should, by all accounts, relieve me of certain stresses, perhaps even feel magical.

This hand takes me places I'm not sure I can go.

I'm a crooked puzzle piece. Magazines babble g-spot stimulation and indiscreet vibrators while the only way I can get wet is by thinking of a man who . . .

Do I not deserve to be treated as an equal? A being with a brain, and the willingness to use it?

All I ever wanted was someone who paid me cerebral attention as well as physical. Yet, my fantasies demand the opposite. The very thing I need is all that I abhor.

"God, you're so pathetic."

My slit trickles, anticipation rekindled but for a moment. Yet as the heat comes, I will it to recede.

I'm thinking too much. It's possible everyone feels this way when they hope to orgasm solely to shut the world off.

Or maybe I'd be okay if I'd never been raped.

"I hate you!"

"Yeah? Good!"

I turn off the TV.

The End

Mania for 1 (Only Human)

WHEN YOU'RE MANIC AF, the only thing to do is live.

Out from an Uber where Terick told you about Rumi and the beggar who threw a book in the fountain that didn't get wet, where Terick told you he was just as heart-broken as you which he knew because you stumbled into his car trembling wet from tears falling from and on your face like rain, out from an Uber that went ten blocks further East than necessary because fuck it, it's 3 AM and your driver was just as sad as you and, after all, you're only human.

Out from an Uber into a diner bursting with life at 3:48 AM. Lizzo pumps through the speakers, everyone is drinking milkshakes, munching fries in their little toques living loud and long despite Coronavirus and/or the impending apocalypse.

Meanwhile in the tiniest washroom in the world, a pretty white girl washes her hands/says she served you at that Greek restaurant a few nights ago, and at first you say, "No," but then you remember that was when your sort-of sugar daddy took you out a few weeks after he bought you that $800 painting on a whim and you admit to her you're having a shit night and she's nice about it.

Back at the bar, you wonder if sugar daddies are worth it for someone like you who stirs up so much drama, you may as well eat it by the spoon.

You just wanted to watch *Hedwig and the Angry Inch* and show your landlord a song from your musical plus enjoy cheese and wine and cuddles. Instead, you got a fullon-triggerfuckfest ending with you on your knees in his office and not in a sexy way, breathing through another tidal wave, learning that the secret to drowning is
BREATHE.

Now, it's 3:52 AM, walnuts in your pocket, and none of this will make sense, but who cares, you'll go home to your cat with her adorable nose and sad, little eye infection, and this mania will pass as does everything, as with this madness so with the world, and you know you're not Bipolar because it only lasts for hours, days, once in a while months, but you know you're not Bipolar because you always manage to sleep. Indeed, these fits are exhausting. You get high on terror and drunk on panic and, before you know it, collapse so far past giving a fuck like the days when you ate shat and spat in victim mode.

Give yourself credit: it's been a while since you swung this hard and you KNEW you were on a swing because of that leap into Hell four nights ago and those fun visual hallucinations next to the toilet ("Were drugs involved?" asked your sort-of psychiatrist, "No," you said, "I don't do drugs anymore", and that didn't seem to satisfy her, but at least you both agreed the Lamotrigine's working—or it was working until tonight.

Maybe you took it too late? Maybe you're up too late. Maybe you shouldn't have gone over there in the first place.

Maybe you can't blame yourself for everything.)

You KNEW responding to your landlord's advances was a bad idea, but . . . he'd been to A-Fest! He liked the Hold

Steady! He drove a Tesla and wore a hat. Plus, it felt like you'd known him in multiple lives and like an IDIOT thought he could improve your life with mentorship and self-development and allowance and/or free rent instead of fingering you up the ass and pressing all of those buttons that so quickly turn to bruises until he says this "probably isn't good for you" and you spin so hard, you're soon shaking on the floor asking him for an ice cube because DBT is the bomb.

There's rows of Tabasco sauce and guys in jackets too nice for this diner and lonely cups of coffee that may just be content. Oh, the joy of a 24-hour diner! (You honour the sacrifice of the sad sods on the nightshift.)

This is the joy of The Big City; there's always a nice place to break down. Somewhere's always open even after your heart is closed.

Life might be okay as-is, but you can still have the guts to try to change it.

I dare you to imagine a future better than your past.

For now, this egg sandwich is enough. The mayo is spicy and "Call Me Maybe" crackles on, three girls shout the hook, sans fucks, the guy next to you at the bar with the way-too-nice coat claps, and I remember this isn't you, it's me, I probably don't know you and possibly never will, but maybe reading this, you figured out what it was like to be me at least during a fit at 4 AM and maybe like Terik reminded me I can remind you we all hurt in our own special ways and we're all special, and we'll all find our way, or maybe not. Maybe you should just wash your hands, drink, write at the bars of diners at 4:14, thank fuck you brought your laptop tonight otherwise you may not have survived.

I hope through this absolute shit night and wicked cruel blue light I was able to channel love through time and space.

It's okay not to make sense, break down crying in an Uber or cab, make mistakes (e.g. encourage your landlord's advances), regret it, swear to do better but fuck up like all those fuckers said you would, shake it off, get seriously into Taylor Swift, go dancing 'cause let's face it you should really go out more often, plan new dreams, resuscitate old ones and hope, and heal, and hurt, and cry, and laugh, and trust we're worth saving even when we're fucked.

After all, we're only human.

The End

These Are the Things
I Want to Scream

I AM MORE THAN A WHORE
GIVE ME BACK MY MONEY
FUCK YOU
I NEED HELP
DON'T TOUCH ME
I SAID NO
I'M SORRY OKAY
I'M ALLOWED TO MAKE MISTAKES
STOP BEING SO MEAN
I AM A HUMAN BEING
HOW COULD YOU FORGET ME
WHY DO YOU HATE ME
WHY DO I CARE

WHY DON'T YOU CARE MORE.

C E Hoffman

Soulfuck (novel excerpt)

WILL FACE/HEART/SOUL/MINDFUCK YOU ON my bloody, bloodied sheets.

It will be the best of your life, and you'll forget me at 2:15, get a scone/career, and

I'll still be here.

Why did I need anyone to tell me I'm good (at anything)? Good is inherent in all beings!

Why did I think I'd save the world when the world will clearly save itself?

FUCK you, Lady Liberty. Fuck YOU, Monsieur Fraternity.

Get stuffed, Pursuit of Happiness/Adoptable Currencies.

For shame your shame, for I AM NOT A COUNTRY, and murder's moot on the Milky Way.

God BLESS the bitchless, proletariat rich by their own means, GOD bless the vagus nerves who swerve n' squirt sexy, streaming tears of joyblisscomradery, perhaps useless under oppressive white supremacist oligarchy, but oh-so infinite I can't give a fuck because all the beautiful is DONE. Kaput. Wah-wah-wahhh. I need not do anying, I could die and be okay. I might live out these harmless days shaded under trees cuddling commercial comedies, CRYING because I LOVE how words feel.

Once Upon a Patriarchy, I wanted to be real or seen or heal. I would've begged some skinny bitch in skinny jeans to say my WORDS ARE SEXY, slip a publishing deal between my legs, and one day, I may yet receive the clitkiss head trip/kick, but even if no one knows (my name), the world will bloom, chart stars, and dance to rock-n-roll foreverandever Amen.

I will fuck the thousandth steaming abyss to get my typewriter fixed. I will learn to walk (in heels), rent cars (road trip!), and buy ribbon, learn to say when I'm pissed, and piss standing up for fun.

I will hump poles, scrub pots of congealed cheese, smile at strangers, pop my knees, all in one just, lusty stab at nobility, for I am beyond and below, I am no/everything.

I'd love to touch you in a way that touches you, but

I Am Enough, I am past You/Me.

Everything's Free once you break from the cage, and no, I dunno who warps the bar or sets the stage, but I suspect it's everyone, a sleepwalk while we're awake.

I dunno why time travel takes an eternity or seconds slide by like headline searchlights, always, always searching.

You are allowed to forget/reject me. I am entitled to fail/age. Success is a basic human right like clean water, big hearts, dense calories.

Perhaps success is simply this: snatching the light only you can see.

You can leave me behind. You can live free of fear.

You can call it a comeback, even though I was never here.

Amen.

My Right (Of Passage)
(novel excerpt)

To SHAVE OR NOT to shave—that is the question.

To wax or not to wax? So is my predicament.

After all, I'm happy enough as a shooter girl, and shooter girls can keep whatever secret they want behind their panties.

Then again, my intention was always to strip, and I've been waiting too long to let it slip through my fingers on account of moralistic encumbrances.

I've saved enough pretty little bills to spring for this most ludicrous luxury of a stranger stripping me bare, but:

1. "Yowch!" and,

2. Why is a bald pussy a prerequisite to strip?

Pussies are sexy, period. Pussies are sexy, even on their period! What's hair got to do with it?

It's the idea of waiting in some ironically Zen waiting room with crisp lighting and pots of lucky bamboo, then, "Yowtch!" and having to ice my cunt for 24-48 hours prior to any extraneous/elicit activity.

Yes, I'm being hyperbolic, but the idea of a Brazilian freaks me. Like, what if it's proof of something? Proof I've sold out/my soul? What's next, makeup? Yeesh!

I opt to shave. It's more frugal, and this way, I can work tomorrow. Mike said my Mary Jane clunkies are fine for the stage as long as I get new shoes soon. Stick it, Prudence!

First, I must trim.

Baby poufs of hair scurry 'round like tumbleweeds. I think of razor cuts, bumps, ingrown hairs, pubescent shame, and force myself to stay positive. I make my reality, dammit! And I will make a smooth shave.

Gone are the days of bountiful bushes and lush armpits. Long ago is the dare of no-hair-don't-care. My pixie cut's growing into a fancy mullet, and no, I will not don a wig; my feminist pride is too persistent.

You can take my hair, but you can't take my heart.

Snip, snip, snip. Thank fuck for D-Fluff (brought to you by our sponsor, Lush). I promise myself this will bring more sensation when we all know it numbs us out. Fake boobs, bald cunts. What's left for us to feel?

So, I'm squatting in my landlady's tub because my bathroom's shower stall will scarcely accommodate this Goliath task.

This five-blade razor leaves a weird residue that reminds me of aloe vera pulp squeezed right out of the plant, but since it's coming out of a razor instead of a plant, I'm creeped.

It shaves off surprisingly easy.

"Bye, bush!" I call down the drain. "I'll see you soon."

Is that true?

I'm up to my ankles in mildew doing a backwards half-bridge.

I kind of like the look of my shiny, bald Venus. It's nostalgic, not just for my childhood, but high school (And Jr. high). I shaved way before it was cool. Then I stopped right before hair "down there" got cool again.

I'm somewhere between my ass and perineum when I hear the door open.

Shit!

"Uh, Shirley, is that you?"

It is Shirley, and she's halfway up the stairs. Thankfully, she stops there before she gets a great show (for free): Little-Miss-Stripper-Wannabe with strawberry shaving whip smeared on her nethers. Lady Luck all out of luck.

"B? Are you in my bathroom?"

"Yeah, I had to use your tub. Sorry I didn't ask first!"

"Uh . . . kay." She says "kay" in that "God, you're weird" way that has proven to me time and time again it is impossible for me to stay friends with women.

Maybe that will change now that I'm on even turf. Maybe sluts can only befriend sluts, and same goes for sex workers.

I'm proud of my shave job until I see little red specks of defeat along my bikini line.

Yowch, indeed.

Being a girl hurts.

And shaving is more trouble than it's worth.

First Date №3

"*Maybe you have to let go of who you*
were to become who you will be."

—*Carrie,* Sex and the City

THE GIRLS LOOKED OLD for twenty-four. The second set was lit. It seems humans do what they do simply to do it. We all have that splash of stupid, angry, ugly fear.

I wish it was socially acceptable to play with your tits in public.

Why do I have to be colourblind when rainbows are beautiful? Bob Marley did it first. Anyway, my knees hurt, and I prefer giving blowjobs on your back.

In other news, people discuss the fit of their shoes in the chill room. I am sober. That one girl is a doppelganger of that lesbian from Edmonton, or maybe that was here and she's herself.

Whispers of the naked world. Salt of the fresh dead earth. Do we write love stories? Will we get what we deserve.

For now, we dance. Three hours later, you will finger me

C E Hoffman

in my sleep, and I will revert to that five-year-old fuckdoll and hate myself for letting you fuck me. I will cry bloody murder and ten hours later eat three spring rolls when I should have had two.

Two hours after, the rain will sting my forehead, and I will tell that nice girl in my meditation group about another strange, quiet rape.

I'm happy for her; her life gives me hope. She's beautiful at thirty-something, has a cat and a Guess purse, and told me all about the fresh innocence of a first kiss on a first date.

The End

On Ezekiel Simon Bowery and His Unfortunate Curse

"One night, I sat Beauty on my knee. And I found her bitter. And I hurt her."

—*Arthur Rimbaud,* A Season in Hell

EZEKIEL SIMON BOWERY, COMMONLY known as Ez, wakes up in an apartment without electricity.

Ez is of Korean and English/German heritage, six-foot-one, and runway-ready thin. Picture the prettiest Aryan girl you can. Combine with the sexiest K-Pop star. That's Ez.

He is a 32-year old virgin, though you wouldn't think it, as people throw themselves on him at every opportunity on account of his kind heart and devastating beauty.

To enrapture Ez, it is not enough to be simply sexy or proportionate. Indeed, Ez is saving himself for someone special.

His roommates are up having their first sniff of BFT. He watches with what can only be considered a polite curiosity. As always, they invite him to join. He politely declines, as always. He thinks they are very nice people, given that they let him crash while he figures out what he wants to do with his life.

He thinks BFT looks pretty nice, too, but doubts he'd enjoy its messiest side effect: bleeding.

BFT is a terrible, wonderful drug, with a varied array of side effects including accidental time travel, lucid nightmares, and bleeding from whatever orifice or injection route is used. The hard-core kids mainline into their eyes, which guarantees the best high and the worst comedown.

Since his housemates snort it, they bleed from their noses, but they look very happy about it, so Ez wastes no time fretting, choosing to see poetry in everything.

This is when he walks through an altogether desolate world: The Big City, with all its post-anti-tech revolution trappings. Yet, he waves to the crackheads cracking their knuckles on the steps of what were once shops and museums. He acknowledges the acrobatic amputees and only ever gets shy around the sad suckers inflicted with Poetry Disease (People suspect it's contagious).

He is on the corner of Dun and King when, much to his surprise, he spots a flock of Pretties.

The Rich and Pretty are exclusive to the North Side. Nobody Poor or Ugly is allowed past North Street. Up there, things are simpler. Up there, they still have electricity thanks to friends in high places. And radiators.

He wonders what these young, nubile Pretties are doing on the South Side. Perhaps poorness is trendy again. Ez wouldn't know, for, like everyone else on the South Side, he is without a toaster, a television, or even a phone.

Without looking at them, he has no way of telling them apart. They have matching elocution and probably matching haircuts.

Thankfully, someone more interesting comes along: Momma Meth.

I'm sure you can divine Momma Meth's profession. She

is hard as her nails, and her nails are permanent shellac.

"Hullo, Momma." Ez greets her, cordial as ever. "How's things?"

"Have you seen Raw?"

Ez is distracted by The Pretties, and has to ask her to repeat.

"Don't think so."

"Bitch owes me money." Momma is seldom one for pleasantries. She also has very sharp teeth, which can be very distracting.

"I see," Ez says, tending to talk in three words or less. He also admits that he's a little distracted by Momma Meth's sharp teeth, but Momma doesn't mind. She likes Ez and, like many other people, grants him a backstage pass on all their soliloquies.

"I'm a good guy, Ez. You get me? I only do what I have to in order to survive. It's a tough, tough life in the Big C. Sometimes, I feel like they locked all of us down here like dogs. Ever try to get to the North Side? It's impossible. Almost as impossible as getting out. Anyway. Raw. Bitch. Don't know why anyone falls for her sob stories. One of my boys 'lent' her funds. MY funds. MY money. You understand me, Ez? What right does anyone have to give away what ain't theirs? I'm going to find her myself, and when I do, well . . ."

Ez's greatest problem is he truly wants to be good. No one else seems invested in ethics, but he deeply desires to die knowing he always did the best he could.

Because of this, he is compelled to suggest:

"I could go."

"Go where?"

"Find Raw."

"Did you hear anything I just said? I ain't gonna trust anyone when it comes to getting what's mine."

"Let me go and talk to her," Ez insists. "She likes me. I could help."

"You soft on her?"

"She's nice."

"You're an idiot, kid." But Ms. Meth weighs her options. "Still, a little diplomacy never hurts. You have 'til noon tomorrow. Either come back to me with my money or proof she's dead. I'll accept nothing less. You get me?"

"Raw. Money. Dead. Got it." Ez nods. "How much money?"

She tells him.

Ez almost falls on the cement.

Looks like he's in for an adventure!

All people do on the South Side is get stoned and have sex and go dancing, which is all well and good, but when it's all anyone does EVER, it starts to feel a lot closer to Hell than Earth.

Ez knows Raw well-ish. He knows she wants to be a veterinarian and she wants to be sober, but she knows neither will happen. He knows she once had two bunnies, and their deaths were traumatizing.

He also knows her "real" name and is sworn to secrecy.

And he also knows where her favourite bar is.

I wouldn't recommend many bars in the Big City. Their customer service is lacking. One will, however, take any port in a storm, and in the Big City, the rain seldom stops.

Sure enough, he finds her at That Bar, the one you would forget as soon as you left it.

She looks oddly pretty under the sad glow of cheap solar lamps.

Raw is third (or was it fourth?) gen of Chinese descent. Her parents have been here as long as most white settlers, and people still call her a *****. Ez looks white enough to dodge most racial abuses and is instead flattered by cat calls and other gender-based harassment.

"Hullo, Raw." Ez welcomes himself to a seat. "How's things?"

He can see (and smell) that Raw has blown most if not all her sob-story money on mint juleps, beer, and whiskey. This complicates Ez's goals for the evening. Killing Raw is out of the question, which leaves making money, a task Ez is scarcely acquainted with.

"I've wanted so many things in life," Raw sobs out, long lost in her alcohol-addled haze. She is at that embarrassing stage of the chronic drunk when all they do is talk about themselves, whether or not anyone is listening.

Lucky for her, Ez is.

"You're the only one who's ever cared about me, Ez. Maybe someone cared about me before, but if they did, it doesn't count anymore. It's a past life. Past lives mean nothing. The only thing that matters is what we're doing right here, right now."

Ez feels a hard rush of Love, strong and still and deep, so real, it rattles him. All he can do is listen to this pickled girl's lost hopes and dead dreams. Her hair is a wad of grease, and her nose leaks, but as far as Ez is concerned, she is the prettiest person in the world.

One thing's for sure: he has to save her.

"Money?"

"You have money?" Raw looks alive, ready to rifle through his pockets.

"No, you did."

"Ohhhh, *that* money." Beer dribbles down Raw's chin. No matter how many shots, she always goes back to beer. It makes her sick, but she doesn't care. "I vaguely recollect." She says "recollect" like "wreck colleck."

"Still have any?"

"Nup." She burps a happy booze bubble.

"Momma Meth will kill you. Literally."

Raw thinks. She philosophizes daily, and mortality is one of her oft-frequented subjects. What is death to a girl who barely lives?

"I'm not bothered." She pulls out her stash for another pint of nice poison. Ez grabs the money for a quick count. The total leaves him concerned.

"This isn't enough."

"It's enough for one more round! Join me?"

"I want to help." Ez feels like he's living a love story. They'll probably elope! Raw won't want kids, but Ez is willing to compromise.

"Come with me." Pending matrimony excites him even more than adventures. "We'll run away!"

"Don't feel like it," Raw counters. "Besides. Nobody can escape the Big City. And nobody escapes Momma Meth. I would apologize publicly, but the truth is, I don't care whose money I spent. Booze is my buffer for life's onslaught of hardships. No, no, I will not, will never, apologize. I'm a Solipsist, after all. There's nothing and no one but me."

Ez lacks the philosophical background required to dispute this problematic conclusion.

Instead, he offers another rope to help Raw out of her tar pit.

"What about money?"

"Hmm?"

"Could we make some?"

Raw thinks.

"I am a proficient panhandler. But not even I can work that quick. We would have to rob a bank, which sounds very tedious, and I don't feel like it." Raw lets her forehead fall to the partition. She tilts her face sideways to stare at the remarkably beautiful Ez.

A lightbulb fires up in her head.

"You." She points. "You could make money."

"Me?"

"You." She lets her arm fall.

"I don't know how."

"Have you looked in the mirror lately?"

"No."

Now, if you will permit me, I'd like to take the somewhat fashionable risk of entering a character's brain. If more people read Ez's mind, I believe more people would respect him.

She insists on one more drink. Maybe it's three. I can't quite remember; the hot smell of melting caramel and burning rubber distract me. I smell honey and horror, and the smell is so familiar, and that's when I realize a stranger at the end of the bar is cooking up B.

The fumes are like a memory I have yet to create.

I watch him "pull back the blinds," as they say. He looks dangerously content.

Hmm.

I return my attention to Raw, the woman I am destined to fall in love with.

Her plan is to "whore me out." (Her words.)

I have no idea how one goes about whoring themselves. What is the etiquette of solicitation? How many love stories involve casual pimping of one's love interest?

Ah, but I trust my beloved. She knows the world better than me.

She unbuttons my shirt, ruffles my bangs, takes me outside, and leaves me under the guise of getting cigarettes.

"Hullo," I say to the first (probable) man I see, as per Raw's instructions. "How's things?"

Raw appears on cue and duly pimps me.

She teaches me how to give a blow job, perhaps expecting I've never given one before. As it is, I have, but I never thought I could request payment.

This is a viable career path!

Of course, I could never do it without Raw. She is my rock, my lifeline, my desert wine, my turtle dove, my sweet sixteen, my go-go baby, my Punk Rock and Riot Girl rolled into one.

They say love comes in spurts. Who would've thought dreams could come true? I've been thinking good things about you. I'm a hopeless romantic, and it's so cool to see her tonight. I wanna be your boyfriend, I'll treat you like I should. The world's a mess, it's in my kiss. There's a little bit of whore in every girl, but you. You're my best friend.

The greatest love anthems of the world rattle my heart and soul. She has turned this simple boy into a prophetic poet. Maybe that's how you get Poetry Disease. Maybe all you have to do to be sick is fall in love.

I enter a world where whatever is happening below my nose is inconsequential. My eyes are fixed on Raw, and every time she smiles, I know I can do anything, and I do.

Some customers pay us just to watch me jack off. I'm flattered, and by this point relieved because I'm exhausted, and my lips have this sad, angry ring of blood running behind them, so I tongue the pulsing throb, and for some reason, it makes me think of BFT.

I bid my final customer adieu. The sun slowly rises.

We have money!

Raw gapes at the pile of bills, then gapes at me, and that's how I know she loves me back.

"I can't believe you did that for me."

Of all the bars in all the world, I'm glad I walked into Raw's.

We still have time before our victory march to Momma Meth's, so we go back to my place. All my nice, new friends are passed out, blood oozing from their noses and lips. They all sleep with strange, twisted smiles on their faces. It's pretty.

"Is that BFT?"

Raw is a special girl. Most would pale at a puppy-dog pile of BFT users, but she, like me, understands the beauty of it all.

She picks up an unused piece. It's a shiny, oil-black square with soft edges, like jello or silly putty. They call it Space Magic, Black Bubble, Blackberry Jam. All are accurate.

The square vibrates in her hand, like it knows we're there.

"Ever tried it?" she inspects it in the moonlight.

"Nope."

"Me neither. Want to?"

Why not?

She says she's never done it before but knows exactly how to chop it up to snort. I am very scared but remind myself as long as Raw and I are together, everything's going to be okay.

I gently push the bubble of black up my nose, like Raw suggests.

I pull back the blinds for the first time.

Oh.

NO.

No no no wait wait wait.

Oh oh oh no no no.

I am floor and hands and oh the blood oh oh no no no so much blood.

Raw sniffs hers with gusto; I hear her snort in the darkness.

I don't like BFT. No biggie. I never have to do it again. It's not like I'm signing a contract.

I will only ever take out a long-term lease on love.

The terrible burn calms to a buzz. I see pixies staring at us on top of the fridge. My dreams coming out of the corners to play.

BFT's okay. Maybe I'd do it again. Not every day or anything. But perhaps on special occasions.

Raw grabs me by my ears, and when she kisses me, I decide BFT is as beautiful as life, which is to say, gorgeous.

"I'm going to fuck you now," she tells me.

"Do you want water, first? You're dehydrated."

As far as first times go, it wasn't the most romantic. For one thing, Raw threw up when they switched to reverse cowgirl. Ez had never experienced the sensation of vomit on his testicles. He didn't care for it.

Despite this, they managed to finish, which is to say, he did.

It was so strange to lose that blissful burst of yourself into another, where you could never get it back.

Raw was the first girl to have sexual intercourse with Ez and, coincidentally, the first girl he ever knew to jump off a bridge and die.

Anyone who knew Raw saw it coming. She was, after all, a Class A Fuckup, and an alcoholic one at that.

Ez never expected that walking Raw home would turn into shouting at Raw not to jump off a bridge.

He thought they were very much in love. They were the post-millennial Bonnie-and-Clyde. Star-crossed lovers all set for happily-ever-after-the-end. Life was all blowjobs and daisies. Life was exactly what he wanted.

They were nearly at the bridge. Nearly back to nowhere.

Raw broke free from his codependent hand.

"Are you okay?"

"I have to go."

"We are going."

"It's the bridge . . ."

"Pardon?"

"It's the bridge. It's the bridge!!!" Her trance broke into a fury. She ran where the cars were parked in perpetual stalemate: a traffic jam in overtime.

She climbed over cars, crashed their headlights.

She climbed over the railing of the bridge.

Ez chased her, all the while wondering what went so wrong so fast.

Love stories weren't supposed to end this way.

"Raw? Raw!" Crisis loosened his tongue better than any alcohol could. "What are you doing? Get down from there, please. See, I knew you should have had that water. I'll go get some, you stay right there . . ."

But he couldn't look away.

Raw did look beautiful, wind swinging through her straight, unwashed hair, bangs setting strange shadows on her angular face. If you asked Ez what it was like, he would admit he couldn't hear a thing but his heartbeat, couldn't see at all but for Raw's wild, angry eyes.

All he could do was beg her not to jump.

She jumped anyway, and he watched her fall, black hair dissolved into black river.

"I HAVE TO SAVE YOU!" he screamed into the darkness.

Nobody answered.

Ez arrived at Momma Meth's at 11:06 AM. He got past security because A) he was expected and B) he was harmless. Or so it seemed.

"Ez." Momma Meth welcomed him. "Where's my money?"

The bills were hot in his pocket.

"I . . . don't have it. But Raw is dead."

Momma Meth's laugh was scarier than her scowl.

"You're an idiot. You think you can hide your little princess in a basement and tell me she's dead? Where's your proof?"

"There's no proof. But she's dead."

Ms. Meth knew enough liars to see Ez was telling the truth.

"Maybe there's hope for you after all, kid."

The End

PS, I'm sure you've figured out Ez's curse. If not, I'd advise you to research the fates of his other sexual partners (Mida, Charlie, Heather, Cello, and latterly, V and Shae.)

But those are stories for another day.

Drinking On the Balcony

She's drinking on the balcony
Her eyes don't concern the sights they feed
And her right to turn
into something better
is swallowed with every drip she drinks.

I saw the same darkened eyes today
ever from a different face
Carbon copies of that glamorous shame
plus that subtle slit of hate
when those eyes lay on me.

Will I be strong enough one day
to dare a mirror and say:
"This is good enough.
I'm happy with what I see."
?

She throws glass off the balcony
and hopes she'll make the cement bleed

You'd think she'd learn
Yet she'll return
To the curb for one more drink.

Let It Heal

TIMES LIKE THESE, I bless this godawful life.

Lucky, dammit, I'm lucky. The luckiest, sexiest bitch alive. Lucky to breathe/shit/fuck/die.

Lucky. Lucky.

Alive.

Don't ask why. It seldom helps. E.g., why do I wake up terrified? Terrorized. Why do those moments burn in my mind? Why can't I let shit go?

Woke up at 3, like before. This time, couldn't get back to sleep (Blame the moon; she's full today. There's no statistically notable increase in emerg room visits, crimes, fights on full moons. Try telling that to my mind).

My shit hurt. I wiped, the blood a surprise. The anal hurt at first, sure, but that quickly dissolves into a deep, enduring pleasure far simpler/less scary than the awful intimacy of vaginal intercourse. Anal, for all intents and purposes, is safe. Same with sucking dick. In these positions, I am most likely to feel powerful and loved and at home.

Yet neither make me cum.

My clit trusts no one but me. My lover had a theory the

clitoris is linked to the social response, so that could be why I cry when someone tries to pleasure me with their mouth, when someone tries to love me with their hand, when someone tries to.

Apart from the crying after he tried going down on me (tears for which he held me, tears after which he stayed), there were only two-three strings of sadness:

1- After he came from my mouth and seemed to be falling asleep and I was left all alone in my unresolved pleasures/pains.

2- After the anal when I knew I didn't love him (yet relief—I knew it would hurt less when he left).

3- I'm not sure exactly when, but there was a moment, a virtually insignificant moment, when my heart spilled over with sadness because he wasn't you, you who were cruel and careless with my precious body/heart, you whom I regret talking to about my voices.

3:54 AM.

Interesting note: sex, like alcohol, shuts the voices up. Anger, too, at times. In these states, my mind is happy-hollow, attention in the body or somewhere near it.

Dr. Chabra worried I'd turn to alcohol/drugs to drown out the voice(s), once I finally told her what they said. She validated my agony. It was nice. I assured her I don't drink/take drugs because, though I would do ANYTHING to never hear that word again, I wouldn't abuse myself to that end.

Abuse is never, ever worth it.

I would not shut up with this lover. He claimed contentment with my monologues. Sexy ones, and sometimes sad.

I mentioned Davis. Twice. Him hitting me during sex. Him suffocating me to shut me up. These memories, I keep in pretty boxes under the bed in my brain because lots of girls had it way worse, and it was years ago, and who am I to complain?

I want to get up and move on with my life. I want to be strong. I don't want to be terrified.

Those are not the memories that keep me/wake me up at night. Those are scars you can trace along the inside of my cunt/thigh, and maybe I will cry.

The lightbulb agonies are weirder. Aliens landing. Ghosts that stalk me for fun. Why are they here? Stop asking, "Why."

Why will not solve your problems.

The cat gnaws her wound at night. I cannot stop her, though I try. I tell her, "Leave it alone." Laugh at the irony of my emo cat. I laugh that her and I match. We are both bloody holes. We gape.

Still surprised my ass ripped. That hasn't happened since Davis, and this anal was pure, beautiful consent, the kind of consent that says, "Yes!" repeatedly at great volume with full faculties and awareness of potential consequences.

He was bigger than I like. But it worked!

Plus, I liked that anal was a rarity for him given his size. This made it special—important to me when I sleep with strangers who may or may not be sluts.

It's not that I need to own them, but I like to know we can attribute uniqueness to our experience beyond our individual existence, beyond the simple fact we shared one irreversible, unrepeatable moment, and how lovely it is that, for this moment, we were young and alive and read Shakespeare and had anal and talked philosophy and laughed. That we made sandwiches and drank smoothies, and I stumbled about in that post-anal stupor I so love and so missed. That a cock splashed cum up and down my throat and face. That he loved what a mess I make of spit.

The cuts will seal. One day soon, shits will not sting.

As for the cat. My wretched, wondrous brain. Who knows? Maybe we will never be the same.

Maybe our wounds make us real.

Would life be so bad if it never changed? Is life Hell

either way? I think not. I say, "no." I decide to like life and, as my analyst says, take the very best of care.

In a month, I will pack, and I'm glad because that means this man and his memory will be safe away from me. This time, I will do it right, like I should have done you, you bastard who does not deserve second person. You, Benjamin, are not as bad as Davis, but in some ways, Benjamin was worse because he alleged himself to be a healer.

Maybe his intentions were real. One day, he may yet heal himself and others. As for me . . .

We all get it wrong. At least I am pretty and young, the cat's fleas are cured, and there's one less guy in the world who doesn't have enough anal.

Honestly though, the anal was for me. I have so missed penetration, but my cunt bears a heavy load of memories. My ass is innocent, and if it bleeds, it's okay because it is resilient, as I am, or hope to be.

I want to be the kind of person who accepts life as-is, even if it hurts terribly. I want to stop asking why, do good, feel great, be free.

The nightmares may never stop.

You have to let them be.

Even if they wake you up at 3.

The End

TGIS

THE CHURCH IS ALWAYS lit.

This is where she smokes when the parties bore her and boys don't call. Here, she contemplates the meaning of life, the misogyny of cab drivers, and why Hollywood still casts cis women (or men) as trans characters.

Her silhouette is convincing under this subtle effulgence. The right drunk might mistake her for an angel dipping out on a Saturday night.

This is the first nice Saturday in weeks; it's the end of May. Who says climate change can't change? Now, it's hotter than hell, and frat boys are out to circle their prey, willing or otherwise.

She dropped out second year but hasn't the heart to update her Tumblr. In the altered reality of social media, she's poly, pre-estrogen, and in-study.

Meanwhile, in *real* reality, she can't afford therapy, and all her "friends" use the wrong pronouns after their third drink.

Her counselor recommended she "find a community," but she was never into the comfort of labels or the lie of identity.

She prefers to smoke.

Sometimes, she passes the infamous frats and considers crashing, but she always keeps her head high and eyes straight. Too smart to tempt fate, and too plain to require validation.

She wasn't desperate enough in school to charm the cool kids and isn't about to start.

Not even on the hottest day of May when the rest of the month felt like March. Not even when the Big City basketball team finally made it to playoffs. And not even after she told her latest BFF to drop dead.

This stoop has fast become her firmest friend. Here, she exists without judgement. The shadows are high enough to flatter oncoming lines or tears or bruises.

These steps are the architectural equivalent to her mom's famous spaghetti. These steps are the closest to home she can get.

Who cares? Better loneliness than shame. Better wondering after faraway sirens than having them pull up at your party. Why risk being stood up when you could order alone in the first place?

A gaggle of girls trips across the moon-flecked dew like confused doves, all creeds and BMIs represented. But all were born of their mothers' bellies, and all will die, perhaps happily.

Their chorus of laughter (a gleeful key) demands one last cigarette. She feels old, or even worse, too young for having not lived.

She's read a thousand books and faked o's for a dozen boys trying to be men, but she has never been in love, been high, or been applauded. She has only ever watched the world through windows.

How does one get in?

Well, her solution comes to her dramatically with a loud *pop*. The lights black out: a dropped curtain. Only the hollow glow from the end of her cig remains. She shudders to think how many asses will suffer nonconsensual gropes under this convenient shield of anonymity. Perhaps on another night, in another life, one of those asses would be hers.

Why should she care if the boys no longer stare or if they ever did? Why should she worry if she walks home alone *again* when that's precisely her preference?

Why risk the "opportunity of night," as Shakespeare once said, for the last two puffs of a cancerous vice? Why wait for the lights to return or for the mosquitoes to bite?

Why not get to bed, or apologize?

Perhaps because, on nights like this, colours seem to exist for her amusement; because cigarettes are delicious, and she doesn't care who knows she cares. Perhaps because she can smell a doomsday imminent the way a butterfly can sense the hurricane he's created.

She stubs her dart. Swallows her pride. Straightens her heel and dials a number from memory—an ace she hasn't played in a long, long time.

"Mom? It's me. I'm coming home."

The End

This Happened №2

NEVER UNDERSTOOD WHY THEY called it The Big City. It may be big by North American standards, but it's pretty much the size of Shenyang (my hometown).

It's on a grid. North, South. Up, down. Figure that out, and you're fine.

The City isn't the problem.

It's the people you have to watch.

I came to the Big C to be a guitarist. My mom breastfed me rock n' roll; it's my bread n' butter, my heart n' soul, the altar on which I spill my blood freely. All I needed was a guitar to ream on, a mic stand to lean on. And maybe someone to listen.

It was inevitable I would room with other musicians. The problem? Musicians are dicks. We're messy, loud, obnoxious, self-centred, and of course, destructive.

It was one of those Saturday nights I wanted to GTFO for all the FOMO, but my roommates were too proud to invite me out for drinks, and I was too proud to ask.

I had three roommates at the time: a bassist (Blues), keyboardist (Covers), and lead singer (Goth) who claimed she was signed to a NY label, though I never saw her play a single show. All her band appeared to do was blow money/drugs in Partytown and jam up my Facebook feed with slutty selfies.

I didn't like her. Frankly, she annoyed me. Of all the self-centred musicians I ever met, she was the worst. As if just because she was a natural blonde with natural Ds, everyone should worship her. She hated to realize she wasn't my type (I'm into brunettes, and I'm gay).

This girl was not the kind to stay inside on a Saturday night, which is why I freaked out when I heard her scream.

This was not the sex-positive porno scream you'd expect to emanate from a singer's bedroom on a Saturday. This was a scream from a horror movie when the blonde finally gets what's coming to her.

She crashed out of her room. I've never seen so much blood. It was like someone dropped a bucket of paint on her arms. And the paint just kept on gushing.

She was the spitting image of Carrie.

I screamed, "What the fuck did you do?"

She screamed, "I fell!"

"Bullshit!" I screamed back—but dialed 911.

They said the ambulance would be there in ten minutes.

An hour later, they showed up.

I learned how to make a tourniquet and applied so much pressure, I thought I'd break her wrists.

"Tell my mom I love her."

"Shut up!"

"Tell my stepdad I love him, too. We don't always get along, but I love him. I do."

I'd never seen her like this: vulnerable, heartfelt, fainting from blood loss. Under all that vampire makeup, there was a scared, little girl with regrets and problems, just like anyone.

After they carted her off to pump her with who-knows-what, I walked down to one of the many bars in Little Italy that advertises Ramazotti or Stella Artois on their patio umbrellas, ordered a I-definitely-can't-afford-this-but-what-the-hell cocktail, sipped until my lips were sore, and contemplated life. And death.

Mostly death.

My mom always told me to lighten up. I was suddenly urged to call and share my woes. Twelve hours ahead meant it would actually be an appropriate time to talk. On a normal day, she'd be painting on the patio listening to the Violent Femmes or the Ramones, smells of oil and coffee and kitty litter.

I'd confided in her so many times, I could predict the whole convo in my head:

Mom: Sweetie?

Me: Hey, mom.

Mom: Wait, wait, I've got paint on my leg. Wait! There. How are you?

Me: I'm okay.

Mom: What's up?

Me: Nothing. What you painting?

Mom: Nothing indeed. What's up?

Me: Well. Something happened.

Mom: You okay?

Me: Yeah, yeah, don't worry about it. How's the weather?

Mom: The weather? Really? Come now. Spill.

Me: Well . . .

After regaling her with my ridiculous misadventure, I knew she would never react like most moms. No warnings or guilt-trips or lectures. She would have simply said, "I'm so sorry that happened."

And somehow, that would be enough to calm me down.

I didn't call. I finished an I-am-at-risk-of-overdrafting-my-account martini and thought about blood. Who knew that much blood could get sucked out of such little arms.

That's when I realized I still had some on me. I rubbed it off, furious, halfway to drunk. This was not the Saturday night I had hoped for.

Normal, happy people ordered drinks at other tables, immersed in their happy, normal lives. Girls walked by, pretty vain and pretty. Everyone seemed to be having a good time except me and the homeless guys.

My Goth-Rock roommate returned from the hospital the next day, trussed up and untrustworthy. I knew her tale of an unfortunate fall onto an unfortunately situated knife was heinous bullshit and took it as a personal sleight since I was the one who saved her life (The paramedics helped too, I guess).

The bassist and keyboardist were clueless. Then again, they didn't have a clue on anything.

"So," was my confrontation while she poured a huge cup of black coffee.

"Hmm?" She almost ignored me completely.

So much for the transformative power of near-death experiences.

"Look." I was not the kind of guy to push, and here I was, pushing. "I'm glad you're okay . . ."

"Why wouldn't I be?" She made a point of chugging even though the coffee was probably piping hot.

"*But*," I continued, "we have to talk about it."

"Nothing. Happened." She dumped the remaining grinds from her cup and didn't bother to wash it down the sink. She dropped her dirty mug on the counter without any intention of cleaning it. She stomped back into her room and slammed the door.

No Thank You. No apology.

She had to be a cutter. Why else would she be so ashamed?

I'd never heard of cutters before I moved to North America. Hell, I never even heard of depression. None of that stuff made sense to me. Why waste time hurting yourself when everyone else is out to get you already?

I fiddled with my guitar, but inspiration remained elusive

unless I was working with others. It helped to have someone bounce ideas back and forth. I liked playing catch with creativity, and catch is a tough game on your own. Not impossible, but lonely.

Could I swallow my pride long enough to knock?

Knock-a-knock.

"Hey . . . ?" I accidentally-on-purpose tilted open her door.

Her room, unsurprisingly, was a mess. I wondered how one person could own that many clothes. All black, no less. She had a ridiculous assortment of hair sprays and body sprays and tiny cases which I could only assume stored make-up. The dresser, mirror, vanity, Queen mattress, floor AND closet were overrun.

I remembered a Hindu friend who told me a myth of Lakshmi when she visited the home of some worshippers to leave them a gift, but their house was so cluttered, there was no empty surface to leave it.

If Lakshmi ever entered my roommate's room, she'd have had a meltdown.

"Hey . . . ?" I tried again. After all, my roomie was liable to suffocate under the mountains of unwashed clothing.

The closet was huge, way bigger than the one in my room. I tried to rack my brain for how long she'd lived in this place. From the state of her room, she wasn't about to leave any time soon.

I don't know what compelled me to walk into my roommate's closet. Call it curiosity, bravado, idiocy. All would be true.

The closest went deep. As a matter of fact, it opened all the way into another room.

I clawed through a tunnel of overpriced fabric and missing shoes to be birthed into what could only be described as a dungeon.

As far as dungeons go, it boasted decent decor. Red,

velvety walls, polished chains, and an impressive collection of paddles, several of which had dildos for handles.

Oh, and my roomie was there, failing very badly at picking up a corpse.

I've done things I'm ashamed of. I've used the n-word. I've bitched about bitches behind their back. My first bf had to come out without me.

But I had never considered an offense as terrible as this.

"GET THE FUCK OUT OF MY CLOSET!" was her greeting.

"Quite a closet you have!" I commented. "Whips, chains . . . MURDER VICTIMS."

"SHUT UP, PRICK!"

I can't believe I was going to ask her to help me with lyrics.

"Give me one reason not to call 911 again and this time tell them to bring you a straight-jacket."

It was surprising to see her give up so fast: on trying to lift the corpse and trying to fight me.

"It was self-defense."

We sat cross-legged amongst the kink while she explained why there was a dead guy in her closet.

"I'm a dominatrix, Zi." (That was weird to hear. She'd never called me by my name, and I'd never heard my name in the same sentence as "dominatrix.") "Though I prefer the term 'Disciplinarian'. And I am in no way obligated to justify my profession. Frankly, I love it. People come to me to release their tensions. Most of the guys who see me are quite sweet. But this one . . ."

It was the first time she referred to the corpse, and I suddenly remembered there was a freaking dead dude next to me.

"I almost never, ever book with strangers. But this guy was recommended. He wanted knife-play, no restraints. We agreed on a safety word, discussed boundaries . . . next thing I knew, he had the knife in both hands and . . . he attacked me."

She brandished her arms as evidence.

"I'm stronger than I look. But he kept stabbing and stabbing, and even though my arms took the worst, I really thought I was going to die. So, I fought back. Better him than me, right? Got him right in the neck."

I wish she'd omitted that part.

"So, this is the part where you judge me, right? After all, it's what you do."

"What's that supposed to mean?"

"Oh please. I may be a bitch, but I'm not an idiot."

"Yeah well, you're not exactly easy to get along with."

"I know." She looked a little glum. "I'm a control freak. That's what my stepdad always said. But being a bitch has its perks."

"Yeah. For one thing, you're the first person I've ever yelled at."

"Really? I yell at people all the time."

"Believe me, I know."

We smiled. We were sitting next to a smelly dead guy, and we actually smiled.

"So, you gonna help me move this or what?"

So far, nothing that weekend was ordinary.

We waited until nightfall, which made everything seem so much cooler and scarier.

I wrapped it in garbage bags; we tied bricks on its feet; she called a cab and paid extra for silence.

We dumped the body off the bridge. And yes, that was much harder than it sounded. She didn't do much except say shit like, "Support the head!" which made no sense.

When that body finally lunged off the ledge and I watched it disappear, black on black, into irretrievable darkness, I wondered about my own body and where it would go when I was gone.

She cried. That surprised me. I cried, too, which didn't

surprise me at all. Sometimes, the weight of life (and death) gets to you. Sometimes, there's nothing you can do but cry.

Next obvious step: get drunk. We slammed back Jack while she ignored every guy's pickup lines. We sang Britney Spears karaoke. We played Mario Kart at the arcade bar.

She paid for everything, which seemed fair, considering.

On the way home, eyes shiny, guts groaning, I imagined calling my mom again. I could picture her on the patio practicing Tai Chi, smiling when she read the Caller ID.

Mom: Sweetie?

Me: Heyyyy, mom . . .

Mom: Are you drunk-dialing me?

Me: Nahhhh . . .

Mom: *laughs* Nah indeed. Having fun?

Me: Kinda. Like, I kinda, um, disposed of a corpse today.

Mom: Are you kidding?

Me: Nah . . .

Mom: Are you okay?

Me: Yeah, yeah. Don't worry about it. It's no big thing.

Mom: It's a big thing to me. You know I always want to give you the space to be yourself, but that doesn't mean I don't want you to be safe. Please be safe, okay?

Me: How? How do I be safe?

Mom: When you're going to make a choice to do something, hold your hand to your heart and ask yourself, "Is this dangerous, or is this safe?" Your heart will tell you.

Me: I love you, mom.

Mom: I love you, too.

I woke up hoping it was all a dream. But then I saw my roommate curled up beside me, arms bandaged, breath pungent from last night's whiskey. She was snuggling in my armpit like the cat back home did.

I had the weird impulse to rub her ear like I would a cat's. Believe it or not, I did, and believe it or not, she seemed to purr in her sleep.

My head was full of happy aches. Despite the hangover, I woke up feeling a little bit invincible. We ditched a corpse last night, and there were no repercussions.

Until we got a finger in the mail.

In the Big City, you don't have to worry about police. Police are just there to harass . . . well, I'm not sure who they tend to harass; suffice to say, it was never me.

It's the Others you have to watch out for. The ones who make their own law and tend to kill each other.

She took it reasonably well, considering the bloody appendage was addressed to her.

"They're sending a message," was all she said when we sat up on the roof, a very gross package between us.

"Who's 'they?' What's going on?"

"I don't want you to get involved."

"I already am!"

Above us, the sky opened.

She quickly lost her patience, as ever.

"Just fuck off, okay? Don't take it personally. I don't let people get too close. It's messy."

"You're telling me." I pointed to the finger which was poetically pointing at her.

She kicked it off the roof in disgust.

"Smart," I commented.

"Christ, you have no idea what I'm dealing with. That wasn't just a bad date. Someone sent that guy after me, and I guess they know I got rid of him."

"*We* got rid of him."

"Oh, I'm sorry, but I don't quite remember you taking a stab a la *Murder on the Orient Express.*"

The rain clattered all around us. It should have been cleansing, but I just felt wet.

"My mom always says the hardest thing in the world is to let people in. It's the hardest, but it's also the best."

"Well, you can tell your mom I only need to help myself."

"My mom's dead."

"Oh."

"She died suddenly. Heart attack. Right after I moved here." The words floated so far above me, they couldn't be the truth, but they were. "My dad's never forgiven me. He thinks it was me leaving that killed her."

"Was it?"

"I don't know. Maybe."

Her lack of sympathy didn't surprise me as we watched the rain.

"My point is, life's short," I said.

"Original."

"I'm serious. If you're in a jam and someone offers to help, you should be grateful. There are loads of people out there in dire circumstances that nobody gives a shit about . . . and I need someone, too. Did you ever think of that?"

"No," she admitted, "I didn't."

In the space where a normal person would offer an apology, we sat in awkward silence. The rain calmed to a drizzle, and the drizzle died into drips. We were awake in the wake of all the unsolvable bullshit making up our sad little lives.

To think, last week, I was bitching at the bassist for never flushing.

"Look, Melodrama . . ."

"You know that's not my real name."

"I'm shocked."

"Do you want to know my real name or not?"

When she told me, I tried not to laugh.

"You know, I like Melodrama. It suits you."

She tried not to laugh, too.

"Yeah. That's the problem."

We decided to run away. There was no sense waiting around for some crime coalition to catch up with us. We figured they'd have an eye on the trains, and a cab would be too conspicuous.

"What about your band van?" I asked.

"It's strictly for show."

"What do you mean?"

"There's no engine in it!"

We decided to hitchhike. She bought us whiskey and protein bars, and we were on our way the next morning, infused with the solidarity that can only come from two over-qualified fuckups taking a second stab at life.

I'll admit I was excited. I thought I'd stay in the Big City forever. Cut a record, go on tour, buy a house, and prune up in the North End with the Pretty n Rich.

Turns out, I was due a whole other adventure.

All I took was my guitar. What more does a musician need? I figured Mel 'n me could start a band once the Big City was behind us. She wasn't the strongest vocalist, but I honestly loved her lyrics.

It was no wonder she had to get the hell out of dodge. We made our way through Partytown, and everybody knew her, even the bums. She was one of those local celebrities, which meant a lot of people probably wanted her dead.

Nobody noticed me.

That's when I realized I didn't have to leave. As far as anyone was concerned, I was another tag-a-long. A loser. A stranger.

Anonymity meant I was truly free.

All the same, we made it over the bridge, onto the highway, past the veritably infinite traffic jams until we reached a shoulder that appeared promising.

Now, there was nothing to do but wait.

Morning broke into day. It was suddenly hot, and we hadn't brought water. We peed in the ditch. Got bored playing word games.

Car after car went by, and every time we stuck out our thumbs and smiled, we were ignored. You'd think at least one of Mel's friends would recognize us, but it turns out popularity only gets you so far.

Our shadows got longer and longer.

To kill time, we talked about music.

"Did you guys have a gig coming up?" I tried to pretend I was remotely interested in her band.

"Nah, not really." She stuck out her thumb in vain hope a ride would materialize. "You?"

"I'm sort of, um, between bands at the moment."

"You're pretty good, you know. I've heard you practicing."

"Don't flatter me."

"Seriously! I would've invited you to jam with us, but ..."

"But what?" I bristled. "Am I not cool enough?"

"No! We don't have a guitarist in our line-up. Just an 8-string bass and electric cello."

"What ... ?"

Another car rolled by without consequence.

"Dammit," She hissed at its tail lights.

"Were you really signed to a New York label?" I inquired, wondering just how stupid I looked giving a thumbs-up to every trucker who passed us.

"Well, I could have been. But I said no."

"Oh please. What struggling musician would turn down a record deal?"

"First of all, I'm not struggling. Second of all, I turned it down because the pervert demanded an untraditional method of shaking hands, if you know what I mean."

"What, like a fist bump?"

"Jesus, Zi."

Honestly, I'd never had so much fun in years, and our road trip had yet to begin. She still annoyed the hell out of me, but now she felt more like a sister than an enemy.

She never said so, but I assume she felt the same way.

Fun is, of course, fleeting, especially under a hot sun. Bitchiness became the prevailing mood, and we were just about ready to find another way when a super sexy car stopped for us.

It was some kind of vintage something (Leave me alone; I'm not into cars). It was a nice blue and super sleek, like it drove right out of a Grease movie.

"Greetings, friends." The driver tipped his hat like a gentleman from the 40's. He was black and cute, and I was weirdly attracted to him even though he wasn't my type.

"Whatever," replied Mel, back to her usual resting bitch face. "Can we get a ride or what?"

"I'd be happy to help you both out, but I only have room for one."

It sounded like a line, but it was true. His backseat was stuffed with files and what oddly looked like old typewriters, most of them blue, like his ride. I wondered if he was a collector of some kind.

When fate throws you a curveball like that, there's nothing you can do but laugh.

"Thanks anyway," said Mel, sans smile.

"Are you sure?" The man looked more interested in us than Melodrama was in him. "I have a business proposition that may interest you both."

"That's no help to us if you only have room for one." Mel suddenly brightened up. "Hey Zi, could I sit on your lap?"

"I'm 6'4", Mel. I hardly think that'll serve us."

"I could come back and get you after I've delivered this young lady," offered our pseudo-saviour.

"Mel." I gestured for an aside. "You should go with this guy."

"Fuck off."

"Traveling with a guy will only slow you down."

"Zi . . ." Mel half-protested, but we both knew she'd go on without me.

I hugged her hard and took the opportunity to whisper, "They're looking for you. Not me."

She was crying and smiling, which were very rare states

for her face.

"Thank you. For everything."

As I watched them drive away, I held my hand to my chest and asked, "Is this safe? Or is this dangerous?"

My heart answered,

"Safer. For her."

That was good enough for me.

Who was I kidding? I hardly knew anything, but of two things, I was sure:

1. Rock n' roll is my heart and soul.
2. The Big City is my home.

Turns out it's even hard to hitch a ride if you're a guy on your own. I had to walk all the way back, and by the time I made it, I had a strange, scary feeling, like someone let the cat out and forgot to let her back in.

I went into her room. It was, of course, a mess. I had to smile at all the useless perfumes she left behind.

I closed the door on my way out, as if in respect for the dead.

"Hey, is she in?" wondered the keyboardist when he saw me leave her room.

"Yeah." I was getting good at lying. "But she doesn't want to be disturbed. I think it's the flu."

"Oh shit." The keyboardist had a phobia for getting sick. "Cool, cool." He ran from the kitchen.

I poured myself a cup of ginseng, then second-guessed my healthy choice for a visit to that same bar I'd patroned the night my life became interesting.

I had a Sex on the Beach or something else ironic and figured my mom would be pretty damn proud of me.

If only I could call.

I still had my guitar on my back. Pathetic, I know, but with Melodrama gone, my Gibson felt like my only friend.

I tried to remember what I did before moving into that fateful musician's apartment. Roomed with students for a while. They were all stressed and boring, and their photos on their Tinder profiles were five years younger and fifteen pounds lighter than accurate. Before that, I was the guest at some Korean lady's place. She was a single mom with two ridiculously pretty kids. She swore one of them was a boy, but I couldn't tell the difference between the two of them.

When I finally took my rightful place as a renter among fellow musicians, I was certain that house was the launchpad of my career. Surely, I would unearth keen collaborators, creative communities, a place to play.

Ha. Ha. Ha.

Expectation truly is the root of disappointment. You can never ask for more than what you pay for and may as well be grateful for whatever you get.

I left a very shitty tip for very shitty service and went home dehydrated but nowhere near drunk enough to pretend I was happy.

I thought of Melodrama. I thought of my mom. I didn't have a clue where either of them were but only hoped they were safe.

There was this really nice alley next to our house, coated in the most colourful graffiti. I often walked that way when I was feeling lonely and homely, and I did so again, holes in my coat pockets making me feel like a far less cool Richard Hell.

"Hey," said a shadow, "got a light?"

"Uh . . ." I feigned a search in my pockets. I knew I didn't but wanted to delay the conversation in the hopes this shadow could rescue me from my pitiful existence.

I guess, in a way, he did.

I didn't even see the knife. At first, it just felt like I bumped myself on a table edge; I think I even said, "Oof."

Then the shock gave way to the pain.

It was like he was hate-fucking my chest wide open. Hot, hot heat from the tip of the blade to the deepest pits of my body.

When he pulled out, the world went cold. Searing tingles mingling with silent tears.

I've never felt anything like it. Except for music.

I'm sure I fell, but I didn't feel anything. I expected to be stabbed again and again until kissed with precious oblivion, but I guess this guy was efficient—or disappointed I didn't put up a fight.

As I bled from my mouth, I thought I heard him say, "You can thank your friend for this."

Mom always said life is no good without friends. She also said to love with all your might, because how hard you love is a sign of how well you lived.

The assassin left as quickly as he came. I'm pretty sure he took my guitar.

I heard footsteps so very far away, starting at a trot and breaking into a gallop. Except these feet were coming straight towards me.

"Zi? ZI!"

It could have been her. Or maybe it was my mother. All I knew was it was someone who cared.

I felt warm hands wrap around my terrible coldness, but there was no pain anymore.

"I came back for you. I thought . . . oh my god . . . oh fuck . . . I'm dialling 911, okay . . . ?"

They said the ambulance would be there in five minutes. It never showed up.

The End

First Date №4

"*Because, sweet friend, you and I are like that red wall. It's a good idea in theory but somehow it doesn't quite work.*"

—*Carrie,* Sex and the City

PINCH MY CLIT OVER my pseudo-silk kimono, the same kimono I bled on that time we fucked on the porch.

Summer seems so long ago. The memory of our love is (almost) enough, no matter how far you cross the line into emotionally unavailable.

No matter how celibate, we're fucked.

What if it's not the thought that counts? What if I really need your hips on my hips and hands on my hands and lips on my lips again and again and-

I figure this is the best way to get excited for work.

This is my first date by the hour; before, I've only done overnights.

I wish I could reduce myself to someone who wants to fuck. The problem? I want to fuck *you.*

I doubt you'd pay for it if you could, and the bank

account beckons, so what can we do? If I could serve tables with a smile, I would, but like that Iranian woman I met on the bus said, "You are on a different path," and I must follow it, no matter how scary or exciting it is.

I will slip on thigh-highs, warm my ass in his BMW, and bid his tongue explore. I will pray to God(dess) his bedroom boasts favourable lighting so my stretch marks remain invisible, and thank fuck, I can fuck for three hundred bucks a pop.

I will fuck my way around the world and, more importantly, do so with love. I will birth a billion baby creations, fingers crossed some sweet sod will pay me to do it, but for now, I am indebted to the power of my pussy and all the responsibility that comes with it.

Do I wish you and I were compatible? Sure. Romance is my chronic condition, but singledom's where we really learn.

I will log off Facebook instead of hoping you'll respond to my flirt; I will comb my hair one more time and rub my tits while my heart beats with the wisdom of the earth. I will go wherever the world needs me to be and love whoever is willing to be there with me.

(I just might have to pretend he's you.)

The End

Dead Beth

THERE'S SOMETHING BEAUTIFUL HERE.

Is it the cracked angels, the graffiti on the crypts? Does death turn dirt poignant?

Is a graveyard really sacred, or is that another myth so the living feel protected?

Could I find faith in the lies of honest men?

I think of the corpses resting (rotting, more likely) under me. They remind me of that day Dad took to me to the fair and I got cotton candy on my shoe. Would blood stick to my sneakers, too? Can rotten flesh get sticky in the sun? Does it turn pink and bubble in heat?

Childhood memories mate with the essence of death, which, in a weird way, makes sense.

"Fuck this," I remind myself. "You're a man. Act like it."

I'm not here to fantasize on the macabre.

I'm here to bring flowers.

I scratch my tattoo sleeve (nervous habit). I dedicated that whole half of my arm to her. Every flower, every swirl, every letter etched into my left bicep is for her, homage to a name I haven't said out loud in years.

I stare at my boots, half-expecting a chunk of cotton candy eyeing me with fervor.

For a second, I forget where her tombstone is, which is stupid, considering how often I visit.

I scratch my arm more. It reminds me of track marks and Intense Orgasm condoms and sniffing stuff from tin foil. I think of the tinsel on Christmas trees, dog shit, my mother and father.

Dad's dead, too. Mom may as well be.

It's better to forget these painful facts of living.

But all we want to let go has a way of resurfacing.

Wind disrupts my cheap bouquet. The daisies already wilted on the walk. Who cares? No flower could compare to her beauty.

What was her favourite flower?

Shit.

Lilac? Tulip? Peonies? I never paid attention.

All I know is it wasn't roses. She hated those. Said they were cliché, provincial, reeking of sentimental bullshit.

Even amidst my sullen, solitary confinement, I have to smile. That was my girl. No high heels or hand-kisses for her. Just dark, dark makeup and dark, dark clubs and big, badass boots that usually went past her thigh. She was amazing and angry and never took no for an answer.

Down to earth right until she was buried under.

Her smile left nothing to be desired. Her tongue left little to the imagination.

I can't remember her lipstick brand, but I'll always remember those kisses. Kisses that hit me all the way down my throat.

Those lips like candy, now spoiling the ground with sugar.

"Fuck this."

I turn back the way I came.

Then I turn back again.

I'm losing sight of sanity. I know her tombstone as soon

as I see it (Christ's sake, I carved it, myself), but it swims in my vision, an effluvium of unreality, singing songs of vertigo and mistakes, the regrets we can never, ever atone for.

The daisies slip from my hands. They fall to the earth in slow motion, reminding me of chickadees and snow cones and ugly liquids in beautiful bottles.

She never wore a scent. That, I know for sure. With pheromones like that, who needs perfume?

My knees find the ground, too. I didn't notice I was dizzy until blades of green tickled my chin, and I have to laugh, or else I'll start crying again.

I roll onto my back, my nose at the edge of her name, dates that should mean something but are meaningless to me.

The carvings mock me, and she mocks me through them.

"Silly boy," she says. *"What's done is done. The past is the past. Get over it."*

She always loved to tease. Against her balcony with her cheek pressed into my chest, at a party with her fingers making hell out of my temperance, or in the middle of dinner when she would hint a kiss, only to pull away for a sip of a drink almost as dark as her lips.

I'm not crying; my eyes are swimming. The flowers are crushed under me. Now, they belong to the mud, dessert for the bugs nibbling my girl's pretty knees.

I like the feeling of losing something beautiful.

I'm not crying, it's just tears. Pieces of sadness packaged into convenient, salty drips, pooling over the edges of my tired eyes.

When was the last time I slept?

Will my tears help the grass grow?

Would she be proud to see me here, a pathetic, pitiful mess trying to make the best of a miserable situation?

Could she ever forgive me for being so weak?

Could I ever forgive her for being a manipulative, lying,

tempestuous BITCH?

Salty liquid calms to a drizzle. I think of playing baseball with my dad. Home runs. Picnics in the park. Cotton candy sticking to my fingers.

Some things we forget, like names and dates, what dress she wore when, but forgetfulness is indiscriminate, and we have no more choice in what we remember.

Certain moments stick, no matter how many times you barter with gods or devils or scientists. You can pop pills, shoot anything anywhere. Bury your demons as deep as they can go, and they always float to the surface. And they never let go.

I'll always remember what it was like to watch her die. How her temples swelled and her eyes popped, turning yellow from white. Every night, I hear her crying, *"Stop, stop, I can't..."*

She never was able to get out, "breathe." Only *"I can't, I can't...,"* until she could only gasp a skeletal groan, and then, when my hands closed harder than I thought they could, there was no noise at all. Only her eyes screamed.

My thumbs pulsed. I thought my wrists might break. I remember her scent, fresh like rain, honeydew sweet.

I remember how moist her lips were.

How they tasted like cotton candy.

The End

February 24, 20XX

IT DOES NOT START with grapefruit juice.

Or Turner Classic Movies.

It doesn't start with indigestion or Calla Lily floral essence.

It starts with a black man driving a cab who said if you're doing no wrong, you have nothing to fear.

I tipped him 22% and decided to be fucking fearless.

He dropped me off at the wrong hotel. B and I found each other in the parking lot. I wanted to kiss him, but he opted for a hug.

He smelled good, and we held hands.

It would be impossible to tell you everything. He told stories about paranoid mushroom trips, NDEs (mostly on boats), alcoholism, the nightmares he had on medication to help him quit cigarettes, how his dog chased rabbits in his sleep.

He smoked since he was fourteen. Drove tractors since we were six. He taught his kids if you kill ANYTHING, you eat it. And though he still used the f-word (not "fuck," "fxxxxx"), I could tell he was a good person. Good enough to hurt, to love, say sorry, and grow.

He gave me the $700 up front to "get it over with." I don't remember if the first time was before we found *Some Like It Hot* on TV or after. I do know we made out on the couch. He carried me to the bedroom like it was real, and I guess it was.

He went crazy (though I say so myself) from my mouth, almost shocked by how good it felt. He loved that I licked his balls (well, I loved it too).

His cock was huge and curved left.

Then it was spicy perogy pizza plus Thai chili wings at Boston Pizza. That's when he admitted he was going to be admitted to rehab. After which, he said, "I didn't want to tell you that." He pointed to the beer at the table. "I don't even know why I ordered it."

Then stories of all the antiques he's found flipping houses.

I cannot explain how you can become a couple for twelve hours with the right person. I think most people just need someone to listen to them, so I did, and a part of me fell in love with him, and a part of me still is.

He watched TV/flipped through his touchphone while I lay my head on his chest. There was more sex then and more before bed. He got close in my mouth, but I said that'd be extra, so he left it (until the next morning, that is).

As for the night, I barely slept. How ironic he needs the TV on to sleep and I need total silence. I kept thinking of the last five minutes of *Stage Door*, a movie I'd never seen before, and I wondered why they were so sad about their friend getting married.

It was too hot to cuddle. I woke up in the night with painful farts—the pierogi pizza was a definite mistake. These are the joys of being human, i.e., not a convenient sex object.

I think I got ten seconds of REM. When I woke up, he was gone for a smoke and brought me green tea from the continental breakfast. Cuddles, cuddles, kisses all the way down to breakfast, where there was grapefruit juice.

I wanted waffles, but there were so many kids, the iron was in constant use.

We flushed four condoms, and when he came in my mouth for that extra $100, I didn't swallow or spit, just let it dribble out my mouth as I moaned him home.

He drove me home, kissed me goodbye, and here, I am, a brand-new prostitute.

The End

Loveslut

I never thought I'd fall for you.
I never thought it would hurt the way you do.
I never thought it would hurt.
I never thought.
There is something about brains fused followed by bodies. As much as I want—nay, need to be alone—LEAVE ME ALONE—I need—nay, want a kind body to lay upon. Hands to hold and face to cum on (jk—I never o from oral).

A cough or cat scratch. Bump on lip or leg. Cig or vape. Crying your name while I masturbate. Or just crying.

There are nights when I can't without thinking of you.

There are nights when I can't.

Do I not deserve someone to kiss, some cock to suck instead of fuck because I want to take it slow?

He was beautiful, but he wasn't you. He could never love/hurt me the way you did/do. Still, a girl's gotta eat/emote in the arms of someone new.

I am messy and broke. If you don't want to hear from me DON'T CONTACT ME why not leave me be.

Can't you see I'm trying to exist?

Don't you know I am learning to be human?

My To-Do list is full of financial assistance, the polyp on my uterus which I like to think was your parting gift, friends and fucks, rent and groceries.

There is no time to do you, too.

I am a b r o k e n mess. I will get through this. I never want to see you again

(unless . . .)

(and less.)

I smell like man's cologne like I used to before I fucked for free. I miss convenient lies. I miss having someone to miss. Loving myself like you never did.

I forget you're still a kid. Which must mean so am I.

There will be other men, women, humans to rev my engine, spark my plugs, etc. There will be other guys with great arms and soft lips who indulge in occasional vices.

THANKS FOR REACHING OUT

BUT I MEANT WHAT I SAID:

One call won't fix this.

I am starved for love and, one day, will gorge but for now ration my masochism. One day, my Venus will pass her eclipse, and I will learn what Love really is. I will spoon-feed self-respect, ponder the past, and won't cry; nay, I will smile for all learned and lost, how one little year b/r/o/k/e me and shaped me into whoever the hell I am going to become.

I wouldn't know how to love you if you never hurt me.

I wouldn't know how to love.

I wouldn't know.

xo

What I Wish I Could Write On My Bumble Profile

I am a flawed, desirous being.
I am broken and bloody and sometimes bleeding.
No What's App, no Snap, no IG
Just DBT, BPD, and (Complex) PTSD.
The only thing instant is my desire when I see
Some shirtless stranger who maybe, just maybe
Might be fit to risk the danger of my fire
Some cutie who may be the boot to my mire
The virgin to my pyre.
All photos are real, unguarded, untouched
I sincerely hope your cock is uncut
the reason I only have one photo of my smile is
'cause my eyes go wild when my teeth are bared.
I'm new to the city.
And I'm scared.

I Could Have Danced All Night (My First Orgy)

Ten people fuck in front of me.

I am struck by the beauty. Here is a world where pleasure is free, where clothes are dropped along with shame.

When I was chitchatting with these normal, non-naked folks in the living room, I never expected they would transform into these erotically sanctioned goddesses and gods. Who would have thought the marketing manager of wherever was a real-life Venus de Milo; who would have thought we are all beautiful and remarkable?

There is so much rolling on and off and away, it's hard to know anyone's role or place. There is softness and hardness and condoms and saliva, girls on top and girls below, a rhythm that becomes collective, a hum from the earth, one big love, one slow fuck for the world.

Yet all the while, I know I'd fail to fuse with the All. Spanks abound, which would trigger me to hell, and there's simply no time to explain what I like, which is almost impossibly soft (and equally rough, and even more loud). I'm better off not getting off, sticking to kisses and whispering in the ears of women how hot they look when they cum.

I make out with the only other single—a male friend of the hosting couple who turns out to be a lot more aggressive than he looks. But then C**** and T**** ask if I want to follow them downstairs, and I do, and Mr. Single comes, too, and soon, I'm watching him cum into a flavoured condom in her mouth while her lover makes love to her gorgeous curves.

I kiss them all in turn. Her hair is soft, her breasts are soft, and her lips, her lips . . .

The Host comes down to check on me; as the only unicorn and a newbie, I reek of innocence and, by proxy, vulnerability. We mash our mouths together, and I say, "Wrap your arms around me."

I want to be held close. And closer.

He leaves to find The Hostess, and I return to my role as spectator, humbled by the art before me. Black on white, man on woman, stranger on lover on human. I tell them they're all gorgeous.

(The best part of a good life is you never have to lie.)

Upstairs, Mr. Single and I munch on yogurt-covered pretzels while everyone else gets stoned in the garage. Now that I am nearly alone, I will dance to "Beautiful People" by Ed Sheeran, in love with my Self, the heart that guided me here, and the soul that always brings me home.

It's been so long since I stripped, but the moves slip out of me as easily as the wetness I know has soaked through my thong. All I need is to be in the midst of this energy, and my body eats it up as my soul feeds on this song.

Sex is the music of the body. Love is the sonnet of the soul.

Me and Mr. Single discuss rising rent prices, and The Hostess appears, still in her cop uniform.

"The Host told me he got to make out with you and touch your boobs. I didn't get to do that yet!"

"Well," I smile up at her, "You're here now, aren't you?"

As we roll around on her kitchen floor and our Venus

Mounds melt as one, grinding and groping and ready for more, and Mr. Single records us, I realize you can fall in love with any moment and anyone. It needn't mean more than exactly what it is: this. Life. Living. Kissing a woman you just met, but feel like you've known so long, you forgot her.

Passion is a vortex. You get swept up and sucked in, and before you know it, almost everyone has gone home except the guy who passed out (probably on Ketamine). The remaining couples have on their coats, but when The Host hears of how me and his wife moistened the insides of each other's mouths, he decides we need to take it upstairs for a final goodbye.

The purple of their room. The thump of the speakers. The mirror on the ceiling. The art on the walls. The Host and Hostess are so close to making love again, and everyone else takes off their coats and slips back into the honesty of their skin.

I do not know how seven people can squeeze perfectly onto one bed. I don't understand how mouths are puzzle pieces, but all of us seem to fit. I don't get how women can tear the world apart when they cum and build it back with one gasp.

One cry. One kiss.

When I watch him ram her from behind. When I watch him choke her, when I realize pronouns are insufficient when attempting to describe an orgy.

I'm on top of The Hostess, her breasts, her hair, her lips, vibrator between her legs, her bones on my bones, her flesh on my flesh, her cries in my ear as she finally cums after fucking like an animal all night.

Now, I'm kissing a woman whose name I don't know. Someone was going down on her, but I don't know if they still are or not. I only know her breasts flying around like her hair, her mouth wide open in a perfect O, and me on top of her, our bodies bursting with bliss.

I fuck her, finally free to let loose my love on the world. This is where we transcend. The point of no return, and the point to which we all return.

She taps out. Neither of us came, but that wasn't the point. I am full within and without.

When I waited in line for the bathroom to pee, before people even began to explore their hearts and minds and bodies, my tight frame thrummed and hummed and purred, engine revved by the mere proximity to anticipatory passions. I was flushed with the rush of humanity, knowing that lust offers the same surge of dopamine as really good ecstasy. Same sweat. Same pushing pleasure and rising waves that never quite crash or break or last.

I don't need touch. I just need you next to me.

I don't need to be loved. I just need to know love exists.

The night became morning long ago, and when the last kinky kids go home, I watch my hosts make love one more time while I lie beside them in bed. I whimper their whimpers and moan their moans, a reflection like the one on the ceiling. And soon, her and I kiss again, and my legs wrap around both of them, and I surrender to the rhythm not of one, but two.

When they cum on top of me, I am at peace.

People are meant to be here for each other. We can choose our boundaries. We have rights to our Yeses and Nos. We are responsible for our development, our desires, our choices, and their consequences, but connection is inevitable. Whether or not you admit it, we are one, in the heart or the flesh.

(6:35 AM.)

Maybe the more we learn to love ourselves, the more we can extend love to others, and the more we'll all act like this life actually matters. Because I really believe it does. Why else would I tear up because she was so gentle when she stuck her tongue up my cunt? Why else would I stare up at my dark

reflection when I'm pretty sure they're both asleep and repeat to myself I am the most alive I have ever been, and I'm so
glad I survived all the times I wanted to die, and sometimes
tried to.

I leave them so I can sweat out these feelings in the guest
room. Before I can sleep, I have to wash some of this love off
my face, and while the cold splashes down my cheeks and
neck and breasts isn't quite as satisfying as the shock of the
shower before I popped my threesome cherry, it's enough for
me to wake up to that sexy, sweet person looking back at me.

"Hello beautiful. I love you."

(The truth will set you free.)

When Eliza sang "I Could Have Danced All Night" in
My Fair Lady, she was really singing about sex. It could be as
explosive as an orgy or as delicate as a kiss. But the tenderest
of feelings occur in uncovering something new and knowing
you as a human are destined to discover the most precious
kept secrets of the world, the sort of mysteries that become
even more special after you solve them.

The End

I Am He

WE ARE ALL WE are all we are all we are all we are all we are all we are all.

Fuck anything that made me feel small. (Do you want me anymore? Do you want her more? Is my tummy too big are my tits too small?) Freaks Are Good, as are we all; I don't care if you're fucking her and I know you are.

That's what Free Love is: free enough to not give a fuck.

Freaks Are Good. Love For All. Black is Beautiful, blah blah blah, but all love's washed out by the drugs, and the druggies don't look sexy, or happy anymore. How can I condone Oneness with the bum spit on the street guts leak outta mouth—no no, I need to Be Here Now; this is a nice party with nice people, Freaks are Good, and We Will Change the World.

I know you are fucking her and instead I will OHH-HHMMMMM, practice conscious breath. Half my friends are Zen, 50% are anarchists who talk like they want to be black, and I don't really want to be anything, but I like the parties. I like not paying rent. I like washing my hair in the sink, and I don't like stealing groceries andandand.

Epicentre.

Oneness.

I contemplate my toes/stare into the abyss.

I don't have (real) friends. I hate dropping acid, tuning out, and coming down/up. Sometimes, I wanna go home, then I feel like shit having the option. You say I can't connect to the greater all 'cause I want to iron my hair, wear heels, and eat red meat.

What if you AREN'T fucking her? What if you REAL-LY wanted to discuss Communism in a quiet room? What if Freaks aren't good but FUCKED, and what if it ISN'T okay to be okay, what if okay is awful, what if I won't leave behind anything worthwhile?

Half my friends are going to India. The other half are feminists. Old boys with glass eyes aver it's the end of the world, but for me, it's beginning or maybe it's the same thing.

"I like your headband," someone compliments me like it means something, like this headband is an extension of Me 'cause isn't that what a compliment's about, really; CON-NECT with this reflection of your Self, and I know the right thing to say is, "Thank You," but I stare into space, and for some reason, she stays.

"Are you okay?" she sits. She has little tits, like me. Little tits are in; look at Twiggy, why worry? Why do I worry about my tummy? My hand's on it all the time, people must think I'm pregnant.

Focus.

Breathe.

I look at this person who is another Me; she could be Chinese, or it could be the lighting, but that doesn't matter 'cause race is over; at least, that's what my white friends say, so I say, "I'm okay."

"Bad trips are the worst," she says.

I am gripped in beautiful panic. I hallucinate peacock feathers in her hair—maybe they're already there.

"You're with him, aren't you."

"Sort of." I try smiling. Everyone knows who I'm with; everybody knows *him*. "We don't OWN each other . . ."

"Sure." She tries smiling back.

Silence is only as loud as its awkwardness.

I look at this girl. She's probably a lesbian. Or a feminist. Or pretending to be both. She probably ran away from her parents like everyone else. Everyone except me.

She asks if she can hug me. It's the most real thing any-one's said. The most real any of us have ever been. I don't think I could ever, ever be as compassionate as this, and the hug ends, too soon for us both. I excuse myself with "Sor-ry's" and "Later's" and head for the bathroom, and I hear you fucking HER in the bedroom—SO MUCH FOR COM-MUNISM—so I ditch the bathroom for the stairs, and the stairs become pavement and pavement becomes a payphone.

I dig to the centre of the earth for a nickel.

"Hello, I'm calling to report a disturbance. There's a ter-rible party going on, and I think they're smoking MARI-JUANA and . . ."

What if Oneness is bullshit? What if Oneness and Sep-arateness are the same? Maybe there's nobody here but me, an experience all at once limited and illuminating. I think I've made every wall a window, even though you say all I pro-duce is unoriginal 'cause it's all been done before and I'm a woman.

Well, fuck you. Fuck everyone in your stupid pad and fuck your daddy who pays your rent 'cause you're "above" ma-terialism. I want to go back and tell the nice girl to get out, but it was her choice to get in.

My head swims, spins. I'm a sinner, and I'm okay with it. Freak may be Bad but it's all I got and that's better than fake friends, or bad boyfriends.

The sirens signal my exhilaration. I don't know what I want, but I know what I don't, and we've all gotta start somewhere; better to start with nothing than too much.

I think of the girl. Her genuine smile. Gentle touch. Maybe in another world, we would have kissed and run away to Cuba or wherever; maybe in another world, she's me, but I'm here right now, and I'm nothing and no one, and I run off the curb and hail a cab I can't afford and it's amazing.

I am running off the centre of the world. I am a new beginning.

I am in danger of being extraordinary.

The End

GTFO №1

I F YOU WANT TO get depressed, I recommend the Big City bus depot.

There is nowhere better to witness first-hand the ill effects of broken dreams.

Exhibit A: Last Friday. Ten people waited for the bus. Everyone else was just waiting.

Two off-duty escorts fixed their makeup in the ladies' room, which, like their lives, was in dire need of maintenance.

One girl was white, brunette—the Girl-Next-Door who left home and never looked back.

The second was Korean with a blonde wig—the promising talent who broke so many promises.

They had that look: hard-working, hard done by, and just plain hard.

"Where you going?" asked the brunette after perfecting her lips.

"Anywhere." The blonde curled her lashes. "Soon as that ticket guy gets off his break, I'm gonna tell him, 'Anywhere-But-Here, and step on it.'"

"Yeah." Eden was busy mourning her lack of a straightener.

"I'm sure he'll be back any minute."

Faces safely hidden, they were free to introduce themselves.

"Lolita."

"Eden."

Both used their work names. It was an act of solidarity and distance.

"Want to get some air?" Lolita had one last look at her wig.

"I don't smoke."

"Yeah, me neither."

"You got me."

Outside, the stars helped them pretend it was a beautiful night.

"Remember when the Big C basketball team won playoffs?"

"How old do you think I am?" Lolita pretended to be offended.

"About as old as me."

"You got me. Cig, please."

Eden obliged.

"So." Lolita sucked her second smoke. "Were you at the game?"

"You could say that." Eden laughed. "I was one of the girls the team called to help celebrate."

"Fuck off!"

"I'm serious! I was doing pretty well for myself back then. Man. I've never been so high. Not on drugs, but on life. Those boys were so happy, I almost cried. They all smelled like champagne. Everything did. They soaked their hotel rooms with it. And by the end of the night, I was soaking, too."

Eden smiled through thin, wise lips.

"Looking back, I honestly have no regrets. The bad times were fucking shit, but the good times were great."

"I'm full of regrets." Lolita laughed. "But at least I made it. Man. There're so many nights I wish I could forget. Like that time I came back from Montreal a mess; FYI, boy trouble does not mix well with mental illness. I went home to drop off my bags and heard my roommates talking about uncircumcised dicks. I'll never forget that. There they were, these spoiled white bitches—no offence—with good heads on their shoulders and good careers ahead of them, pontificating on the pros and cons of foreskin, and there I was, dropped out before I got in, off to psychiatric emergency. Again."

Eden offered Lolita another light through the darkness. She gratefully accepted.

"When I got to emerg, there was some deaf spaz threatening the receptionist. Then the cunt shoved *me,* and I just lost it. Man. Most of my regrets involve not punching people who clearly deserved it. I should have wailed on that bitch. Broke down sobbing instead." She felt the earth beneath her boot. "I don't even know why I'm thinking about it. So what, I'm crazy. Everyone is. How else could we have survived this bullshit?"

"We all have our vices."

"We all have our reasons."

"Skeletons."

"Demons."

"Exes."

"And we all have our stories."

Their smiles matched.

"What now?" Lolita asked.

"What do you mean?"

"Where are you going?"

"Oh." Eden was glad the darkness hid her embarrassment. "I haven't thought that far yet."

"No worries. Anyone who thinks they know what they're doing or where they're headed is even crazier than the rest of us. Anywhere-But-Here, man. Who cares where you end up? All that matters is you have the balls to get up and go."

"So, are you going to work when you get to . . . wherever you're going?"

"Probably." Lolita shrugged. "I like it. Guarantees there's someone to cuddle. Helps me afford my meds. What about you?"

"I don't know. Probably?" Eden shrugged back. "At this point, I'm down for anything. I've been a cleaner, a server. For a while, I was in an assembly line making car parts! But I've always come back to sex work. Loving people feels like home, you know? It's taught me the power of No. And the power of Yes. More importantly, it taught me I don't have to be scared or safe or care what anybody says."

"I don't know if whoring taught you that. But living sure did."

For a while, the stars spoke for them.

Eden had to ask.

"Why haven't we given up yet?"

Lolita looked to the sky.

"Hope keeps us going, I guess."

"Hope that the good times will return?"

"Or that the bad won't come back."

"Nah, we're off track. Everyone knows the odds are against us. Optimism can't mean crossing your fingers that your cheque will finally come in. Otherwise, we'd all be idiots."

Lolita had to smile.

"Aren't we?"

"Maybe. But we're also resilient. Resilience means we carry on, even if it never gets better."

"Ha! And all this time, I thought I was a pessimist. But I believe life will improve *if* you work to improve it. Just you wait, girl. When that bus comes, we'll get a fresh start."

"Yeah. It's gotta get here soon."

"Yeah. Any day now."

The most depressing thing about the Big City bus station is the buses never run. You can only wait and wait and wait and hope for the break that won't come.

At least, not today.

The End

Between Lines/Legs

NEVER WANTED HIM. NEVER will. Hated him more than... loved him even more than that and...

I wanted to retreat. Tail between legs. No eye contact. Fist in his face. Every day, I saw him.

Every day, I saw him, I...

Shove my name up his nasal tract. Give it all up. No acting here. No trying to be pretty. No faking any strength.

His smile melted into a sneer, stinky and sticky and toxic. Romantic somethings and friendly nothings turned to shards in my chest.

"Speak of the devil."

Cruel shrieks. Cruel laughs.

The laughter was worst. Winding around me like I was some disease, like touching and taking all those kisses (pulling them, wrenching them from my lips) was the onset of a sickness, like touching and kissing me again would rape the marrow from his bones and leak liquid into his brain.

Never wanted me. Never did. Maybe once in a while, but he'd always find someone else to warm his ribs...

I wanted escape, but those pills didn't quite work, and he

C E Hoffman

stayed tucked safely in my nightmares.

Used to fantasize. Kill him. Shoot him. Burn him. Choke him. Shove needles down his throat or up his ... kissing him (like rape, like love) while he vomited viscera and said good-bye to our cruel little world, that world we swore to fight against together.

"Go and die!" The sadness flashed in his eyes, and I was reminded of what we had been.

But those pills didn't quite work, and I wasn't allowed visitors.

What about scraping his skin? Licking tears, savouring the salt (Just one more time). Hearing him say that thing (just one more time) and ... moan like he used to on the phone when I was shoved in blacked-out corners of my room, cunt a hot rock on my hand while praying no one would hear the dirty words dripping out my desperate mouth. So god-damned desperate. Hear him buck and spray on the other end, so goddamned far away, never close enough I could touch him, let alone reach him, reach that puss-blocked or-gan I so needed to see ...

Could I eat his heart, rape his soul, ruin his corpse, brand my name into his hand just to make sure he'd remember? Make him read me every time he wrote a note, scratched his chin, or rubbed his cock empty?

I wanted to run. Bolt, scatter with broken ankles. Kick up dust, kiss his broken nose, and watch the comets of my love blast off.

Then he was gone, up and out of my life, up and out and gone and hardly ever seen and ... suddenly, I needed him. Just to see him again, no matter how much I didn't want him.

DIDN'T, DON'T, NEVER WILL WANT HIM!

There were so many days (months ...) that went by with-out a word. I'd hear of this girl or that girl but tried not to get jealous because I had this guy and that guy and that girl, too. Separately, we lived in sins. We made memories. We lived them.

There were occasional sightings, like the time we were in the same club and my heels were too high to dance. Kisses, always, regardless of this girl or that guy.

"You look so good today." I was quiet in the face of his compliments (then again, I had a vow of silence that day.) He always used to compliment me before the insults, before the pills.

Then when it (finally) happened . . .

Awkward kisses lacerating skin, but never enough to draw up blood, to leave some humble mark on me or him (like a welt, like a scar), real proof we'd ever been there, or that we'd ever been at all.

Snakes shedding our morals in the light.

So goddamn desperate.

"It's just, it's been so long . . ."

"Shh." He shut me up with his tongue. I sucked the calcium from his skin like I always longed, no matter how sad or empty or wrong it all was.

Kissing down his body:

"Aren't you still with her?"

Head back in self-loathing:

"This will be good for us. It'll help our relationship."

His words like burns on my breasts. Mouth suddenly chalk-dry, desert-dry, no saliva coming up no matter how hard I tried! Scorned kisses on his cock. Fucking him with a dry, angry mouth.

Never wanted him, even when he was in me.

Over too fast. Split from the moment, rushed with those words he used to say to me. The "uglys" and the "freaks . . ." "We went our own ways . . ." "She broke my heart once, then had the nerve to think we could stay 'friends . . .'" "Let me fix your hair so you'll look like a normal person . . ." "You look so good today . . ." All announcing a drought between my legs.

Numbing nerves, cutting beautiful throats in my brain.

Such pretty paintings (lost) in passion, so many dreams (lost) in smoke. That fire always fed our lust . . . determined our love and our hate and the regrets of what we wanted to be . . . strangely absent when our bodies (finally) collided.

That house was so goddamned quiet.

Too far apart, even when he was in me.

I walked around the basement. He went to get water—or to avoid being in the same room. I saw this warped version of myself in the TV. Looked at my body. Wondered if I was burnt up on the inside, where he couldn't see. If my shrunken, slightly damaged liver was working overtime to clean me.

Would I ever feel pretty? When did love become a cancer transferable through the lips?

There was a pebble in my shoe. It ate at my big toe while he walked me to the bus stop.

Never wanted me. He never did. Not even when he was furiously thrusting (finally in the same room as his lust) all the way up to an orgasm shot against the sheets, an orgasm that came too fast and didn't last long enough for either of us.

We touched each other like strangers, like the lovers we should have been with.

Had he stopped wanting her, or had he wanted me too much?

Didn't ask too many questions. Not enough to discover the truth.

Would have loved to end it for good. For one of us or . . . both of us.

Wondered if he ever wondered about me.

Never wanted him. Never will. Couldn't love him, not like I loved this man or the other. He hardly even knew me, seldom ever saw me.

Never wanting to see him . . . always half-hoping I will. I left that city long ago, but who knows? Maybe one day, we'll run into each other, crammed in the corner of a bar, too close to touch, too far away to speak. Or a park with a wife at his side and child on his arm, eyes begging I might grant him the escape he always sought, that I will return to him as the Other Woman to hide under his shame, wrap my sinewy flesh-sticks called legs around his waist . . . finally getting the chance to say, "No, not this time."

Maybe if I could just hear him say it, that thing he would never say unless he was drunk or we were texting or emailing or hiding on the phone, that thing he would never say as long as we were face to face and . . .

The End

I wish I said this but blocked her instead

You best not be with L***.
💀

Yes, I was with him, and I am so sorry-
not only for being intimate with him,
but that you're stuck in his life.
He is a lousy lay and shockingly selfish.
All he cares about is himself and any woman
in the world deserves better,
including you.
I met him early at the train station,
paid for his cab, listened to his songs (all he wants is a
groupie),
encouraged him, celebrated him, cooked for him,
gave him a blowjob. He meanwhile got drunk
within an hour of coming to my apartment
and basically ignored me after he came
(in thirty seconds, by the way; like I said, he's a lousy lay.)
He promised he'd help me study for my final.
He said he wanted to catch up/hear about my life.

He did none of these things.

L*** is a shitty person, C***.

With hope he will improve and you two will be happy,

but if he's still pulling this bullshit after knocking you up

twice,

I doubt it.

We Know How to Die

We know how to die
When stars drop like hearts bleeding out of our minds

The pleaser, the teaser, the bitch on the bleachers
The prude who's too moody to take what you leave her
The old girl who's digging for gold that may keep her

The bed that we buy is the one that we lie in
The boys who we break are the ones we confide in
The girls who we kiss are the ones we won't miss

Though I pine and rely every guy has a price
Each word is a lie, my victory's a vice
Sugar and Spice
Naughty is Nice
Scars won't get us far on this road they call life
When our Johns and our wrongs are too big to deny

We know how to die.

Bitches,

THE DJ RE-MIXED "JANIE JONES," an attempt to bridge dance and punk.

The punks hated it. So did the dancers.

It was the last club in the Big City worth the cover charge (which nobody paid). I got in because I happened to know exactly what the bouncer was doing last Pride.

Everyone was wild. Tek was tripping, Q was lippy, Serval was ecstatic. He stripped down to his shoes long before the police raid.

I'd never seen him so happy or so high.

He dragged me into one of the dirtier cubicles. I was dubious.

"I thought you were straight . . . ?"

"C'mon, man, it's practically the 22nd century!"

That boy devoured my foreskin.

It was too good to cum.

(This story isn't about Serval, but I mention that blow job every chance I get.)

Of course, Ez was at the show. He came in late, like always, dusting off from a long day's work of giving head.

C E Hoffman

I always sensed Ez before I saw him. You can call bullshit, but I knew Ez's pheromones like a gangbanger can sniff out a cop. Pigs are a risk for the head, whereas Ez was a risk for the heart—mostly 'cause he reminded you that you had one.

One time, he stepped on a ladybug and hosted a funeral. Nobody went. Nobody's dumb enough to be vegan anymore (except Ez).

Ez looked young for his age. Thank the pickling drugs, mom's golden genes, his naivety. His thighs were like needles. His jeans were made of duct tape. His boney wrists were oh-so-lickable.

Everything on him was lickable.

His eyes could make a grown queen cry. His hips were ready to slice. People said his cock was perfection, but I had yet to verify.

Christ, listen to me. As if words could make boners pretty.

He was a ride. That's all I mean.

That night, he was busy with a list. I don't know what the list said, or how he could even read it in that perfect darkness, but he held that scrap of paper to his chest like a condom on his heart.

I locked my thumbs in his belt loops.

"Hey babe. Wanna get me drunk?" I trilled into his ear.

He beamed like a trout on acid; I stepped back to admire his teeth.

"You're drunk enough." (Three words: a standard Ezian response.)

"I got a lonnnnng way to go, babe."

I kissed him hard and hot, hoping he'd melt.

The DJ was sucking so bad, everyone was leaving or acting like it. That could only mean one thing: V was back.

The only reason they let V play was 'cause she was gorgeous: a stunning five-three, ninety-five pounds of nubile blonde jail bait.

"Someone should tell that slut punk doesn't belong on a dance floor."

"What?" Ez was distracted by the world.

"THIS DJ SUCKS!" I yelled.

"I LOVE PUNK!" Ez yelled back.

The Ramones came on, clashing against some archaic jungle beat from the oo's.

"The Ramones?" I moaned. "You've got to be kidding. You're supposed to *wear* the Ramones, not listen to them!"

"WHAT?!"

I kissed him again. Maybe he'd choose the same stall Serval did.

I loved that crazy kid. At least, if I'd ever chosen someone to be in love with, it would have been Ez. I wanted to make him squirm, tickle my tongue with his ear, ram everything everywhere.

"Get me a drink."

At the bar, we could (sort of) hear ourselves think.

"Face it, Ez; punk was dead before you were born. You and that shit DJ must be the only people who still listen to it."

Ez admired the blissfully ignorant blonde behind the turntable, his smile a dreamy, wet fish.

I was instantly jealous.

"You know her?" He knew I meant: "You fucked her?"

Everyone knew V, and everybody fucked her. She claimed she was gay, but her condom supply suggested otherwise.

Even if she was a lesbian (WHICH SHE DEFINITE-LY WASN'T), she would have fallen for Ez. That was what made him such an indispensable hooker. Gay, straight, pan, celibate—he could convince anyone to love him any way they wanted. He was any and everyone's type, regardless what their type was. The sloping bangs alone, man.

To this day, I have no idea if he was gay or bi or just plain lost. His mouth was made for sucking, he had perfect bj eyes, but he always flirted with drag queens and drooled at tiny breasts.

But he got boring. Kept to kissing and fingering assholes or cunts. He seemed preoccupied, guilty, gutless—any time he saw a girl that made his zipper skip, he'd play with that damn piece of paper in his pocket, as if the skin of a dead tree could suck him off instead.

V finished her set (thank fuck). She made her obvious approach. Leather corset, scissor-ripped leggings, buzzed from the drugs or maybe the music.

Ez's wrist was too weak to wave. V pointed at his chest, alight with hetero interest.

I was instantly jealous.

"You look familiar. Were you the guy with the Rancid bag that time?"

The kid actually *blushed*. If I could see that under strobe lights, V certainly could.

She was nice. (Bitch.) Asked him what he was high on that night, to which he offered the most hilarious lie: "I'm sober."

The last time Ez was sober, his testicles hadn't dropped yet. You could have cut chunks from his veins and sold them at raves, good as pure. You know what they say: a hit a day keeps the nightmares at bay, except on BFT, the nightmares follow you everywhere.

"I hated your set," I told V, trying to be friendly.

She laughed. (Cunt.)

"Nobody likes punk." She smiled at Ez. It was the kind of smile that lit her whole face. (Slut.) "You're the only person I know with good taste in music."

Ez looked like he had a fresh shot.

"Hey." I fingered his collar. "Can I talk to you? Over there? Away from here?"

"Away from me, you mean," said V.

She was too smart for her own good.

I crushed Ez against the coat check. Wight was killing time near the long-dead payphone, pretending to write a review. I ignored him, and I'm sure he preferred it that way.

Meanwhile, Ez was enjoying the attention.

"You gonna go with V?" I ruffled his bangs so they went the wrong way.

He patted his bangs back, smile still the same.

"Jealous?"

"Jealous? Ha!"

He seemed pleased with my performance but persisted in his bullshit.

"No love tonight. I'm abstaining."

"Abstaining?"

"Yep."

"From sex."

"Yep."

"You are physically incapable of celibacy."

"It's not that hard . . ."

"Tell that to your dick."

He beelined back to V, so hetero-obvious. I trailed behind as his catty, candid chaperone.

V was handing out party favours: penance for her poor attempt at musicianship. Bring the right drugs, and you're everybody's friend.

She let us choose between green, purple, or pink. It was her first peace offering of the night and wouldn't be the last.

She was too nice for her own good, too.

"Stop, drop, n' roll!"

I dropped that pill, alright. I dropped it like a dirty dildo.

It got me all excited.

I wanted adventure, I wanted reality.

I wanted to fracture fantasy with a wrecking ball.

We danced out of the club, singing nonsense (that is, lyrics). I became the perfect machine, void of vulnerability or any other useless humanity, and all the time, my soul raged on, bleeding without release. I asked the stars, "What'll happen tonight? Will anything happen at all?"

I tripped. The sky turned to street, and the street was on my face. I raised my throbbing forehead to discover the source of my fate: a Buddha statue beside the club's entrance. I stared into his saucer plate eyes, crinkled and euphoric, forever frozen in a joy we'd never know.

I kicked that fucker again and again until my toe burst from the inside out.

"OW!" I cried and continued to kick.

"Isn't that bad luck?" V warned from the curb.

"Believing in bad luck is bad luck." I kicked the fucker again. And again. And again. "That damn thing came outta nowhere! I always knew the gods hated me."

"Surely," V hoped, "gods would be more forgiving?"

I was too peaky to punish her stupidity. Instead, I found the clouds and learned the secrets of the universe, forgotten three seconds later as I was so distracted by the dusty, dead stars.

Sky's always nicer than concrete.

I would've omitted that part of the story, except kicking the shit out of Buddha left me with a bitch of a limp, which is not only embarrassing, but important.

My armpits wept. I was getting perfect shakes. Summer was ready to sour everyone's milk, and damn did I want to burn. I wanted to sizzle, crackle, and snap, ram UV rays into my solar plexus.

We had nowhere to go, like anybody would at 1:13 AM on a Thursday night (or Friday morning). Sleep deprivation was doing that funny, buckling thing to my brain, a side effect I thought I'd beaten down in my teens. Brains learn to function on however little food, sleep, or sanity you give them. Only spoiled skulls complain.

My head learned to shut up long ago. Same with my heart. Why either decided to have an opinion was beyond me. The drugs birthed a new me, one I didn't like, because this guy had thoughts and, even worse, feelings.

Empathy is dangerous.

V was prattling on and on about her aspirations as a DJ. As if DJs have any of those! She was driven while retaining humility, so much that she became a person to me, and I really hated her for that.

I was always better at making enemies than friends. More than that, I preferred sex. Why should I relate to someone platonically? Slutting it up is the only way you can connect with another human being.

"Music has more power than we give it credit." Or so V prattled on and on. I was bored; Ez looked apt and daft. "It's the simplest way to tap into the human spirit. After sex, that is."

"What?"

V blinked, her face wet with fireworks. She looked dehydrated, like her lipstick was ready to bleed.

"I was saying music and sex help us connect."

"Bullshit!" I cried, craving a fight.

Much to my annoyance, Ez came to V's defence.

"You don't think so, Judas?"

I flinched at the use of my full name but persisted. "If anything, sex pushes us further away."

"Perhaps it depends on who's having the sex!" V tried to help.

I rebuffed her olive branch. The dopamine release emitted flood after flood of affection, forgiveness, friendship, and other idiocies that only ruin your life and crush your spirit. The drugs scrubbed me with hippie bullshit I was determined to reject. Any trip had to hit me with the perfect rage of cocaine or burners of meth. Otherwise, it wouldn't be worth it.

I wanted aggression. I wanted rape. Somewhere in my mind's eye, demons exterminated pandas and shat in toddlers' mouths.

"What the fuck was in that pill?"

"It's ecstasy," she said, all wide-eyed white-girl innocent. It made me want to hang her from her ankles until her prettiness came clattering out of her pockets.

"ECSTASY?!?!" I screamed. "ARE YOU TRYING TO KILL US?!?!"

"You don't like ecstasy?"

"Where'd you even get any?"

"Well, there's this guy . . ."

"NEVERMIND! The point is ecstasy is death. Ecstasy is the last thing anyone here wants to feel. Right, Ez?"

"It's nice."

"NICE?!?! Who in the world wants to feel NICE?!?!?!"

I had to start a fight; otherwise, I'd give in to the love, and that was the last thing I wanted.

"Um . . ." said V.

"Is that the kind of bullshit you're trying to stir up in the world, V?" I got all up in her face, happy to see her shrink. "Is that it?! You want people to think you're nice."

"She IS nice," Ez insisted.

"Not for long! Just you wait. Two years on the scene, and you'll see this bitch for what she really is."

"If you hated ecstasy this much, you could have just said so!"

"I'm not talking to you, bitch! I'm talking to Ez!"

We dragged him in, desperate for a referee. V was bruised from being my punching bag, and Ez would surely soften my blows.

He struggled for a moment, then conceded. "People . . . love . . . life. Am I right?"

We had to agree. For a second, the hate in my bones went to rest, contentment sabotaging my calcium deposits.

Things were pretty awkward at this point. I considered ditching to find Serval or someone else drunk enough to forget I was such a dick. Why waste time with a pseudo-straight rentboy and claim-gay pussy who looked like she ran away from Pretty Rich boarding school?

Why? Why? *WHY?*

Because it was my sacred duty to cock-block.

I felt a moral obligation to sabotage their fun. There was far more at stake here than my blue balls or my pride. I somehow knew protecting V from Ez would save her life.

I guess ecstasy inspires delusions of grandeur in narcissists.

I was too old to think. Or too young. Either way, I wanted nothing to do with a highly functioning brain. Philosophy was as useful to me as a condom without a reservoir tip.

Now, I wondered, how do you keep two perfect, skinny, sexy hetero humans from falling in love and subsequently having sex? (Or having sex and subsequently falling in love.)

One thing for it: they needed an adventure.

Adventures were hard to come by in the Big City, unless you count breakup angst and overdoses.

So, I said, "We should break into the asylum."

Stupid. The asylum was one of the first medical institutions to shut down mid-revolution. People were too busy throwing pipe bombs (or ducking them) to worry what happened to the crazies. I figured they were let loose on the streets. By the time the dust settled, they'd have blended in easy.

So, we broke into the asylum. Crinkling glass announced our arrival, and Ez pulled V through the window by the roots of her splitting hair. They had a moment when she fell into his arms, as girls so often do, and I severed the moment by accidentally-on-purpose bumping them both, as the jealous one so often will.

"Sorry," I said, trying to be nice. "This limp is killing me."

That much was true. I was hobbling. But there would be no love story on my watch. Limp or no limp.

I don't waste time on morality. If I want to do something or someone, I do it. That's my compass, and it's never lead me astray.

The asylum was awesome, by the way. Apparently, we weren't the first to come up with this bright idea. Graffiti tarnished the walls, including and not limited to, "GET OUT," "HACK A DART," and "IT WASN'T A DREAM."

Puddles of old, murky rainwater made it difficult to know where to go. Same with the clutter of condoms that looked like perverted party balloons, the broken chairs and pyramids of beer cans looking like the craziest museum sculptures.

"It's really dirty in here," remarked V, a pinch of princess showing through. "Why don't we go back to my place?"

"You have a place?" Ez looked way too excited.

"Kind of. There's this guy..."

"NEVERMIND!" I interjected hurriedly. "What's over there?"

I faked curiosity all the way to an ominous set of stairs.

"Truth or dare! V, you first."

I turned to see those two sluts murmuring sweet nothings. I heard, "Confide in me..." and almost saw a kiss.

"AHEM." I cried, high as hell and even more determined.

They jumped to attention.

"What?" they said.

"What?" I said back.

V tried to fill me in. "I was just saying..."

"You talk too much."

That shut her up. I was pleased to see one of my jabs got between her happy-shiny armour. For a minute, I saw the bad bitch waiting beneath, and I liked her.

Some girls just need a push.

"Truth or dare, V?"

"Dare. Always."

"I like you already. Go down those stairs! Stay down for one full minute. Come back and tell us what you saw."

"You don't have to." Ez touched her arm lovingly. Blech.

V was already halfway there.

"It's okay. I'm always down for an adventure."

"From what I hear," I sneered, "you're always down for anything."

She tried to ignore me, but I knew I was wearing her down. She'd sooner leave in tears than in the arms of Ez. At least, that was my plan.

Her tight ass disappeared in darkness.

We waited. And waited. Ez for his blonde beauty to reappear, me for a scream that would announce her timely demise.

Funny, wishing death on the girl you're determined to save.

We waited. And waited.

I counted one minute. Then three.

"V?" Ez called.

Nothing.

"Oh well." I grinned, task accomplished. "Want to go back to my place?"

"Judas!" Ez shook his head in gentle admonishment. "Be nice."

"Why would I ever want to be that?" I dragged his junkie sleeve. "C'mon, let's get drunk again."

"No way!" He marched to the stairs in defiance. "You coming?"

The stairs felt spongey and mouldy and wet. I almost slipped into Ez and idly wondered if he would catch me with the same care as he did V. I wondered how high he was and when I would finally come down to earth where I didn't care about anything.

Much as I wanted to deny it, I was worried about V.

It was dark as hell down there, and while we expected to land on another floor, there was nothing but stairs, down and down and down and down, up to the point where I started to think of Wonderland.

V would make a great Alice. I would, of course, be the Cheshire Cat. And Ez . . .

"SHIT!" I heard him stumble and cry and . . .

"EZ?" I ran forward, which was stupid, because the poor kid had so obviously fallen off an edge or down a hole or . . .

"*Shit!*" I fell with him.

My leg was busted for sure.

On the plus side, we found the basement.

"Ow," announced Ez. Then he called into the still-pervasive darkness, "V? Are you okay?"

"Fuck V! What about me?" I demanded.

Ez helped me up, but still, he bleated, "V? V!"

"I'm okay," she Marco'd to his Polo, annoyingly calm. "I'm trying to find the lights."

"There will be no working lights in this place, you IDI-OT!" My patience was at a dangerous deficit. "Did you forget where we are?"

Before a reply could be given, the lights shuddered to life, suddenly and ominously, and that's when V screamed.

Row upon row of hospital beds, there were kids hooked up to machines, every sad sucker somewhere between POWs and science experiments.

Their heads were all shaved to allow for an impressive assortment of electrodes doing who-knows-what with their brains.

But all the more disturbing was that they had no brains at all.

I moseyed over to one "patient". His morbid haircut reminded me of a sweet skinhead I used to fuck. His eyes were jellied glass. They wobbled in sincere, pleasurable pain, once victim to reality, now freed by insanity.

Once sick with consciousness, cured by incoherence.

I've never seen someone so hot or so high.

That was when I noticed the ridiculous stitches, like someone sawed a hole in the back of their head.

Sometimes, you just know things, like how I knew no matter my efforts, Ez and V were intent to destroy each other's lives. (High-five for assisted emotional suicide.) In that same way, I knew all these sorry souls had their brains stolen for someone else to play with.

"Oh!" Ez stunk up the place with empathy. "This is awful! We have to help!"

V was already desperately tangled in someone else's IV, a dumb kitty-cat dizzy with moral intentions.

"Don't!" I dissuaded her well-meaning idiocy. "Most of them are dead, anyway. Or they're going to be."

It was true. Only now did I notice the bloating blue of so many fresh corpses, so many kids close to their last shit. This was a botched experiment left to die.

"Nobody's just going to walk out of here."

"I have to agree."

We turned to see some old, fat, white guy with an admittedly charming smile. He was handsome in that old, fat, white guy way. I wouldn't have kicked him out of bed, anyway.

"I'm impressed to meet such eager volunteers." His squeaky-clean smile started to make me sick.

"What is this place?" V demanded, almost as horrified as Ez, and almost as curious as me.

There was something weird about this guy. I liked him.

Ez, too, noticed the weirdness. Even V had an inkling.

There was something about his skin. It was—I don't know—bloodless. Like there was nothing going on in him but his selfish thoughts and deeds.

"You're dead." It was only after I said it out loud I knew it was true.

He laughed the deadest of laughs, guilty-as-charged, but guiltless.

"I'm just visiting. Looking for recruitments. You understand. Society may crumble, but Science marches on. Life may end, but death doesn't."

"This is the worst first date ever," said V.

"It's NOT a date," I insisted. "You're a third wheel."

"Not for long." The doctor smiled.

"I have to agree!" Ez grabbed V's hand and bolted back the way from whence we came, his little baby deer legs snapping under the stress.

The doctor watched them go, nonplussed. I comically tried to run, but my leg was a mangled mess, and all I could hope to do was call out to my so-called friends, "Wait for me!"

They didn't.

Bitches.

On the plus side, I get paid really well as Mr. Wick's assistant.

The End

Bass Lines,

I REGRET IT.

    The kiss was bad (but good, which made it worse), and fingering her tiny, hot cunt instead of paying attention to the exits was wrong (though wonderful).

    It's been a while since I had to run. I probably look like a baby deer in duct tape pants.

    "F*****!" screams a not-so-eloquent drunkard when I wriggle through a not-so-comfortable fence hole, V coming soon after me.

    "Where's Jude? Where's Jude?" V sounds like she's crying, but we have to keep running, or I don't know what will happen.

    We run a little longer, just to show we tried.

    My eyes sink into a dismal twilight. I can't believe I'm going to miss another sunrise.

    Ah well. There's always time to make it right. That's the joy of this kind of life: you have nothing but time.

    I readjust in my pants, impressed and surprised by the persistence of my erection.

    It's good I'm a little horny before work. It always helps.

    It's not that I dislike sucking cock, per se. Cocks are pretty in their own way. It used to make me gag, but that was before I decided to write my own story about what I like and don't like.

I like giving the guys stuck in traffic jams a break. I like being able to afford as much B as I need. I like having extra money to sneak into the pockets of friends.

Sucking cock is a small sacrifice to keep living.

First things first: go get Judas.

Then again, maybe that can wait. We need something to eat, some dreams to sleep, a few more kisses, and a little prick of B.

B's always a good idea. On BFT, everything's milkier. Like a bunny on your insides. It's a little creepy when you have to inject it into your eyes, but that's the fastest way, and your eyes end up bleeding either way, so who cares?

"We need to get Judas."

"Yes. Tomorrow. For now, let's rest."

I hold her hand and make promises we know I can't keep, but when a girl cries, I'll do anything to help her stop.

My head should be reeling from all the injustice, but I only remember the bass from her set and her breasts in that corset.

My soul craves greatness.

All I want is sex and music.

The End

And Suicide.

LEARNED A LOT WHEN I turned fourteen:

   1. Avoid puppeteers like monogamy;

   2. Avoid monogamy like anal;

   3. Avoid anal like the plague;

   4. Never say "Kiss me" again; and,

   5. Music has a power people rarely understand.

Eden's in the discs. You spin, strangers hug, magic happens. Reverb carries more weight than any revolution. Music is the antidote to war. A rave is a peace march stuck inside (and sometimes under the stars).

I could talk forever about timbre, major vs. minor, phrasing, beat-matching, transition, (dis)harmony, (re)mixing . . .

But when you're escaping a hospital that was supposed to be abandoned, heels kissing dirt, knuckles sucking thunder, there's little time to say anything except, "Hurry!"

Boys always say I talk too much. Especially about music.

Ez runs in front of me. He waits for me to catch up, snatches my hand, lets go, grabs again, and with my silent consent, drags me into his madness.

We cuddle the pressure, the panic, the sexual tension. My

synapses snap like the lights in a club that feels so long ago, a gig that would have been great if only I was better (or worse) at my job.

My corneas wobble from the last ebb of drugs, ecstatic inside their gelatin.

It could have been a great show. If only I'd been alone. Every kiss would be perfect, every track would be an encore.

If only I could be alone.

"Wait! . . . We need to get Jude."

We catch our breath. Ez looks back to where we were, but Judas has fallen far behind, and our adventure along with him.

Q1. Did he get caught in the clutches of that creepy doctor?

A1. Probably.

Q2. Will we go back to rescue him and become the heroes we were meant to be?

A2. No way.

Now that we're alone, sex is inevitable. Our lips and gropes will get sloppy and obvious, invoking a guilt to numb the lust, increase the self-loathing, and keep me kissing him.

Our mouths stay separate. Silence tries (and fails) to fill the space between our bodies, a chasm of air ready to collapse.

I know I'm a lesbian because cocks always disappoint. But after a night like this, the pills decide everything. When you're this high, there's no such thing as a finish line. The race is non-existent. Life becomes what it always was: touch, love, sound, sensation. Life becomes music.

If only the night/high/songs lasted! I'd love sound and song at my fingertips all day. I'd shit house and eat vinyl for breakfast.

They say life used to be easy. Lonely, awful, but easy.

"Kiss me."

"Come back to my place."

It's a familiar proposition, usually uttered with more

estrogen.

Then again, Ez is beautiful. He's half-Asian, and his black bangs are always a little too long. He is almost pretty enough to be a girl and almost sweet enough for me to trust him.

"You have a place?"

"Not really," Ez admits, black, narrow eyes shirking streetlight. "But I know somewhere."

It's a shooter's den; it smells like the 70's. I step over syringes—some used, some fresh—and Ez tickles my ears with another fib,

"Those aren't mine."

I skip across the floor, a ballerina playing with landmines.

"You never shoot B?"

"Hardly ever," he lies for the second time in twenty-eight seconds.

"I've never. It freaks me."

He likes my lie better, so he agrees. "Me, neither. Wanna try?"

Needles always feel bigger than they are. Same with shits, cocks, and problems.

The hit: immediate, cross-eyed, swift. My eyes bleed; my sinuses spit. Somewhere in the city, someone's touching someone, someone's cutting, someone's Zen. The sweet crush of pheromones and . . .

SLUT.

I always hear it in my head before the high or the bass makes me deaf. Again and again and again:

SLUT. SLUT. SLUT.

Tears mix with the blood. He holds me close, kisses softer than butterflies.

"Shh, it's okay. The first time always hurts."

All my firsts were years ago.

His tongue is my crutch. I'm anchored inside the hurricane.

I feel like starving in Springtime while he's between my

legs.

The rumours are true; he's amazing with his tongue. Fabulous, even. The blood and tears dry on my face, and my eyes are free to roll.

"Oh yes, yes, softer, yes . . . !"

I've never enjoyed this before—certainly not with a man.

Just when I'm about to cum, I hear it again:

SLUT. SLUT. SLUT.

"Stop, stop. I can't."

He wipes off my clear gloss with another kiss.

"Are you okay?"

"I'm great."

"But you're crying."

"Kiss me. Kiss me until I can't cry."

He tries his best. Somewhere between our lips, I find the fire again, and SLUT ebbs away like the tidal wave of drugs in my veins.

His penis is just hard enough, and I'm more than ready, dripping wet. I'm surprised and impressed by his stiffness, considering his blood content.

"Ohh." His moan is halfway to a sigh, raining blood and showered in sex.

I doubt it'll last.

Then again, nothing good ever does.

Tangled sheets bring tidings of UTIs.

It's funny how little I feel. His cock—raw, pulsing, tumid—locks with my vaginal wall. He's in this body, and this body is surely alive, but sensation's dead, and my enjoyment along with it.

I'm hypnotized by splotches on the mattress.

He's in me, but I'd rather talk about music. I don't want flesh grabbed and ass smacked and cheeks hot with vomit.

I'd rather hump a mixing board with my hands.

I'd rather be a person.

I should stop . . .

Is he done?
I should pull out.
He must be close . . .
I don't want to hurt her.
Why am I doing this?
What if she dies?
Like all the others.
I should stop . . .

It hurts, but this pain belongs to the whole world. I claw Ez's shoulders, suddenly invested in our connection, seeking his eyes, urged to find the soul behind them.

I need to pull out before . . .
Ohhhhhhhhhhhhhhhhhhhh . . . !

He's done. I feel it . . . we've exchanged more than saliva, semen, bubbling BFT. Having his arms around me feels dangerous, even though I know . . .

I don't want to hurt her

We rise from the mattress (rug, chair, who cares) to retrieve whatever fabrics were discarded before the mistake.

On the stairs, he thanks me for music and kisses me like I'm responsible for all his good sleeps and better dreams.

"Are you okay?" He worries.

"Always."

"You should stay." He grabs my hand, motions me back to the mattress. "Stay as long as you need."

All I want is to leave, forget this ever happened. I want to leave myself behind with my mistakes.

Ez is too weak on B to force me to stay, but I can tell that's what he wants. Even the nice guys go crazy after I fuck them. Figures.

Now, the aftermath.

Alone, the road, the curb, the clubs. Partytown is still hard and hot and alive from last night while I couldn't be more dead.

I have a vision: a generation immobilized, a girl who

could have done something great, a girl who failed when she should have tried.

Love is a great depressant.

The End

Have You Seen V?
(novel excerpt)

LOVE LEAKS FROM ME now, drops of cum sent to wring sanity from my thong. The leather clothes clasping my body like rubber bands screech, "I fucked him, and I liked it."

Did I?

I only remember the stains. Perspiration and sickness from the gig combine with shameful, human colours—purple like bruises, blue like corpses.

There used to be discs, dancers, risk ... but every night, I lose another chance. Every night, my hymen cracks.

Each fuck is exactly like the first, 'cause it always HURTS.

I thought life was okay. Stealing cigs, peddling pills, making friends in mosh pits.

Whenever the headaches were too much and I was starved for food or company, I could always count on the dykes. I marched their marches, sucked their piercings, and they loved me.

I thought they loved me.

I thought there was peace in music or beauty in depravity.

Now, I see the ugliness. The blemish is not only outside, but in. Cancers creep slowly so you'll ignore them. They

C E Hoffman

make nests for their babies long before you itch. By the time you scratch, it's too late.

I scrape my heel on the pavement.

What did I want to be?

Did I ever consider being anything?

Everyone on the scene is older than me. Nobody knows I'm only fifteen. Or maybe they know and don't care.

Punks gather at the foot of the hill, waste-buckets of slobber and ripped fishnets, death as close as the dawn we deny. We push our penniless pleasures to the last possible moment, not because we're having so much fun, but because we fear the consequences.

I used to find charm in the ironic facial hair and tasteless tattoos. Now, I know life is a waste. All of our clothes are costumes.

I judge my own outfit: thrift store leather, rusty chains, distressed, scissor-ripped leggings that look like something out of a bondage magazine.

I feel so idiotic, I start to cry.

"Why so sad?" A girl in rubber boots reaches for my zits, chewing on a pencil stub or pixie stick. She's left one of the after-hour raves, neon bracelets pathetically competing with the moon.

"No idea!" I sniff between sobs, and I mean it. "I've never felt this shitty before."

"It's just a bad trip."

Life is a bad trip. (Did I read that somewhere?)

The girl happily struts towards her own demise.

For an instant, I'm flooded with romantic impulse. I want to go back to Ez, if not for another kiss, then another hit.

Ez is so nice. Why should sex with him make me miserable? He wasn't bad in bed. Gentle, even—a firefly playing tag with my clitoris. Of course, I couldn't cum, but that's what I expect. Go in wet, come out hungry.

My tears are so thick, I could catch them in my corset. I'd be fine in a few lifetimes, but I've blown all my chances at reincarnation.

I'm going to Hell for sure. There's too much bad in me. I've cheated, stolen, lied. I've lied to lovers, lied to friends.

I lied to everyone; I said I liked it.

The world's a hammer sawing away:

Gottafindafuck Gottagetahit Gottashutthesevoicesup...

SLUT!

SLUT!

SLUT!

THERE'S NOTHING THAT CAN HELP ME!

All I have is an empty purse and an angry chest and tons of friends who don't give two shits if I die or live.

The last time I cried this much, I was shoved through mom's cunt from the safe, sweet womb, hurtled into this awful world.

The pain will pass. I'll be better by morning...

If morning ever comes.

Someone will care. Someone will look for me. There're so many girls I've ensnared with my eyelashes. At least one will comb these vomit-strewn streets. Two weeks from now, they'll be asking, "Have you seen V?"

That, or they'll forget me. Better to bash your brains numb and dumb than suffer the truth.

They'll lock us off and drown us out. We'll starve before learning to cook for ourselves. The shops will finally close, solar panels will fry.

We're a plague, and we're treated like one.

Look at this terrible city. LOOK WHAT I DID TO IT!

"What I did?" echoes my last voice of reason. *"I didn't do anything..."*

Too late for logic, love.

Too late for logic or love.

I'm smothered by the blacks and greys. This bridge is the only slip of red left on the horizon.

It's the bridge!

It's the bridge . . .

GTFO №2

IT WAS HARD ATTRACTING a car when you looked like shit.
Xia did her best to cock her hip, muddy thigh teasing
wind. Her thumb whistled, tilted towards anywhere but
where she was.

Cars zoomed by, leering eyes judging from afar.

She wasn't looking for a date but hoping for a ride.
Though at this point, she'd take whatever she could get.

Her salvation was a battered Dodge Ram. The rust made
her feel right at home.

She tried to get a good look, aware of the risks when
someone is disinclined to reveal their face.

The driver: long, black hair. Dark brown skin. Resting
bitch face. Ironic Raiders hat, plus a toothpick that suggested
an oral fixation.

"Where you going?" the driver asked as Xia stepped
inside.

"Anywhere." This tease was lost on her rescuer. So, she
slammed the door and said, "As far as you can take me, I
guess."

The stranger nodded, too serious.

C E Hoffman

"I could do that."

Off they went, the driver and the hitchhiker, protected by a steel box eating up the road and poisoning the world.

If Xia was lucky, she'd opt for the next rest stop or bus stop or shoulder.

If Xia was lucky, she'd get to the next city alive.

The longer they drove, the more she doubted her decision to get in. There was something inhuman about this trucker-girl, like she didn't know what to do with her skin. The eyes deep-set in her face looked dead with indifference.

"So, thanks for the lift. I had to GTFO ASAP, you know what I mean? The Big City's gone a bad, bad way. I would have tried a cab, but cabs only work when you know where you're going. Not that a cab would ever come to the South Side! Ha-ha! I didn't even think I could get past city limits. But somehow, I got through."

Xia always babbled when she was nervous. Nervous as she was, Xia couldn't tell the whole truth and nothing but the truth, because the truth of how she got out was absolute madness (and best saved for another day).

"Ever been to the Big City?" she asked her driver.

"I haven't been anywhere." It sounded like a lie. "Not 'round here, I mean."

"Oh? Where have you been?"

The conversation ended with a question mark.

Towns turned to highway exits, exits turned to fields, and the fields had a few forevers to contend with.

Xia felt the weight of the Big City melt away with every mile.

She always hung out with a lot of whoevers at a lot of wherevers. This made for a lot of great nights she'd never remember.

Now, she was free to embrace the silence.

Much to her surprise, it was the driver who killed it.

"Do you know what I hate about you humans? You're all

so . . . stupid."

Xia blinked, unsure of either sentence.

Bliss is a luxury only afforded by the rich. Road trips are a breeze when you can afford roomy, leather seats. Everyone else has to stay on their toes, because you never know what madman (or woman) is going to pick you up from the side of the road.

"Sorry . . . ?"

The driver's eyes kept to the highway, but somehow, Xia felt like they were face to face. Her fight or flight response chose, "freeze," and she did, clutching the seatbelt all the PSAs swore would protect her.

"I was sent here to learn love, but how can I when you never love each other, let alone yourselves?! All you ever do is bleed, wage war, and procreate. Even your geniuses are idiots!" The girl's hands crushed the steering wheel. Xia watched them shake. "This world revolts me. All this pitiful physicality. Phlegm. Onions. Divorce papers. Suicide." She broke her nails on the wheel, but the car stayed steady. "Why would they send me to find beauty in repulsion? How can you love anything when everything *hurts*?"

Madness was never so poetic or so sincere. *Was this the end?* Xia wondered. Panties around her knees, blue, bloated corpse stuffed in a muddy ditch? Another MMIW who wouldn't make the news? Another goddamn victim of quiet genocide?

No, Xia told herself. *Your story doesn't end that way.*

"Um, here's good. . . . Or anywhere, really."

"I have tried SO HARD to do good, be good, feel good. I'm done. I just want to get out of here."

"Welcome to the club." Xia couldn't believe herself. Was she really goading a psycho? *Eh, what the hell.* "Everyone wants out. Why do you think I'm running away? The Big City's falling apart—literally! And unlike all my friends who seem content wasting their lives away, I want . . . something.

I don't know what I want, but I know it isn't this. That pain you talk about? It's not all yours. It's everyone. All the time. You're not alone. We *all* feel it, one way or another."

Akshita looked at Xia. Tears streamed off her face. All human imperfections—small eyes, fine lines—dribbled off like stage make-up. Soon, she was porcelain, a beauty too pure to be human.

"Do you have any idea how many times I've tried to die?" she cried; Narcissus cracked, Aphrodite aged from stress. "I try and try to die, but this world won't let me go. They say I can't leave until I learn what love means. But love means *nothing* to me. It never will. It never did."

Xia grabbed the Venus's hands. The car stayed straight on the road.

"You wanna know what love is? It's sticking together. It's doing what you can. Even if it's something little, like, I don't know, picking up a hitchhiker."

She gripped tighter. Akshita gripped back.

"What the hell can I do?" Akshita really wanted to know.

"Just take me as far as you can."

Akshita saw Xia through the tears and, for once, smiled.

Her foot landed like a dumbbell on the gas.

Xia fell back.

She heard the tires sear. She smelt the rubber melt.

The car shot off the pavement. Tires lifted. They struggled at first, then rose into sky, a steady incline like the vintage biplane ride Xia's grandma took her on before she died.

She stared out the window, air a waterfall on her face, breaking pores and cutting dirt away.

The old Dodge Ram crawled its way up the clouds. The harder Akshita pumped the gas, the higher they flew.

The car's hood was wiped clean by all the blue.

Xia would have screamed, but there was no need. Silence said everything.

Breathless in the wake of an agonizing skyline, she stole

one last look at the highway, now a charcoal line splitting through yellow fields.

The Venus beside her smiled, tears all but dry.

Xia: "... Where are we going?"

Akshita: "As far as I can take you."

Looks like they were going further than she thought.

The End

Bloom (Blowjobs)

After a mouth full of fucking
I guess I could tell you about
The bits of skin I left in Gillettes to
which these scars still attest
but I'm bored writing poems about them
especially since
I've got new marks from planting trees and
making a masterpiece mess in the kitchen.

After a mouth full of fucking
I suggest
you wipe spit from your cheek when
your lover says
it was the hardest they came in their life, and
you believe them
happy to be on your period
writing poems about blood/cum/
alternative fertilization

when your borage finally bloomed

so did you
after a mouth full of fucking.

"I don't even know how to be a prostitute. I mean, really, how much small talk is required? And where do you go? And are BJs a must? Because if that's the case, I am so not doing that . . ."

—*Lilly,* Gossip Girl

Thank You

Thanks to everyone at Safe Space.
Thank you, establishments, which will
remain anonymous for my sake.
Thank you, punk shows, gardens and pills.
Thank you, fuck-ups, break-ups, and spills.
Thank you, cats with whiskers and trees with
leaves and dreams with possible meanings.
Thank you, bitches and switches and
therapists. Mobile crisis units.
Thank you, BFFs and uncircumsized dicks.
Thank you, Spotify and comedians.
Thank you, London, Toronto, Halifax, Edmonton.
Thank you, mum 'n dad. Thank you, sister,
uncles, aunts, grandparents (all nine of them),
dogs, cousins, cousins, and cousins.
Thanks, bandmates. The periods that were on time
and the dates that were late. All the magazines who
deemed my stories worthy. All the stories. The guts
and the glory. And of course, the mistakes.
Thank you, bullies. Thank you, fakes.

C E Hoffman

Thank you, servers, cab drivers, DJs.
Thank you, parks. Thank you, subway.
Thank you, Margaret. I am very sad you died before I
got a book published, and I'm very sad you died.
Thank you, Deryk. I'm very sad for those same reasons. ^
<3 <3 <3 Thank you, Lizzy. Thank you, J. <3 <3 <3
Honour and acknowledgment to the First Nations*
in the land we know as Canada on Turtle Island
where these stories were written and published.
*Including but not limited to the Mississaugas of
the Credit, the Anishnabeg, the Chippewa, the
Haudenosaunee, and the Wendat Peoples.
Hugs to my efficient editors and perfect publisher.
Thanks for contending with my alliterations.
Thank you Ryan, aka Some-Sum, a terrific
poet and incredible test-reader. Your
suggestions were valued and acted upon.
Thanks to the guys who ripped me off, pushed my
boundaries, or crashed through them. To the ones I
lost. The ones I loved. All the times I fucked this up.
But most of all, I want to thank myself. For being
through AND raising hell. For living 15 more
years than I thought possible. For keeping calm
and carrying on. (Carrying on, anyway.)
Thank you, soul. For loving and believing in me. Thank you,
body, for letting me live. Sorry for all the times I cut you
and made you throw up, made you believe you weren't good
enough. Sorry for throwing you into the arms of people who
didn't deserve you. Sorry for not thinking ahead. Thank you
for your optimism, and most importantly, your patience.
Thank you, reader. You help me exist.
Thank you, God/Universe.
Thank You.
Thank You.
Yes. <3

And most of all, thank YOU, dear reader.

If you enjoyed this, please remember to
review it on your favourite site.